Tongues and Bellies

The Whole Kahani

Published by Linen Press, London 2021
8 Maltings Lodge
Corney Reach Way
London W4 2TT
www.linen-press.com

A CIP catalogue record for this book is available from the British Library.

Cover art: Arcangel
Cover Design: Mukkteshwari Nagpal and Pratibha Nalawade
Typeset by Zebedee
Printed and bound by Lightning Source
ISBN 978-1-8380603-1-2

About The Whole Kahani

CATHERINE MENON   DEBLINA CHAKRABARTY   KAVITA A. JINDAL   MONA DASH

NADIA KABIR BARB   RADHIKA KAPUR   RESHMA RUIA   KHADIJA ROUF

The Whole Kahani (The Complete Story) is a collective of British novelists, poets and screenwriters of South Asian origin with an array of awards. Contributing to this book are: Reshma Ruia, Kavita A. Jindal (co-founders), Mona Dash, Radhika Kapur, CG Menon, Deblina Chakrabarty, Nadia Kabir Barb and Khadija Rouf. The collective has published two critically acclaimed anthologies: *Love Across a Broken Map* (2016) and *May We Borrow Your Country* (2019). The collective was shortlisted for the Saboteur Awards in 2019.

www.thewholekahani.com

Praise for *Tongues and Bellies*

'Rich, incisive and at times magical, this is a collection to be savoured and cherished. A joy from start to finish.'
— Awais Khan, author of *No Honour*

'But where are you from originally?
This line from Khadija Rouf's story is a theme that runs through many of the stories. Food, identity, loss and the burden of cultural expectations are woven through effortlessly. The best kind of short stories are those that leave you with unanswered questions. This collection of stories does that and more!'
— Asma Khan, Chef & Owner, Darjeeling Express

Praise for The Whole Kahani

Praise for *May We Borrow Your Country*

'A thoroughly modern and lively collection which reaches out across multiple histories and distinctive worlds to capture some of the best in contemporary British Asian women's writing today.'
— Susheila Nasta

'A rich collection…with dry humour and poetic verve.'

— Preti Taneja

'Stories that dazzle with a sensitive brilliance.'

— Rebekah Lattin-Rawstrone

'I thoroughly enjoyed this anthology, loving all the different perspectives within. I was delighted by the variety of character voices within the stories and poems, men and women trying to make sense of their lives and worlds particularly when finding themselves far from the homelands they grew up in.'

— Tracy Fells

'Trailblazers who provide an authentic lens on what it means to have dual British and Asian identity in a time of political uncertainty.'

— Brown Girl Magazine

Praise for *Love Across A Broken Map*

'They eschew stereotypical stories about the experience of the South Asian diaspora in Britain. Instead they reach from Britain into South Asia and back again, tackling universal themes rather than culturally-specific tales.'

— The Short Story Review

'An unsettling collection laden with remarkable stories.'

— Mona Arshi

'There are no forced marriages, arranged marriages, domestic violence, culture-gap issues in this collection. What we do have are darker characters, stories that are gritty, bold, funny and without the stereotype.'

– Reginald Massey

CONTENTS

MEG KOWALSKI'S
BIRTHDAY CAKE

Reshma Ruia

'A Marriage made in heaven' is what my friends called it. I was in the final year of my Ph.D., researching Machiavelli's *The Art of War,* when my supervisor, Dr. Elish suddenly slipped on the pavement outside his house, cracked his ribs and was out of action for the rest of the academic year. Bill was his replacement. He was a few years older than I was, with large, expressive hands and eyes that slanted down at the sides giving him a slightly needy air. He also wore corduroy trousers and a tweed waistcoat that carried the whiff of charity shops and mothballs. Bill was only a Graduate Teaching Assistant so he was nervous about moving into Dr. Elish's office with its single aspidistra plant and framed prints of Florentine flora and fauna. He preferred our seminars to take place in a quiet corner of the college cafeteria. He always ordered a mug of tea and a slice of carrot cake. 'Cakes are my weakness,' he'd admitted on our first meeting. The tips of his ears went pink at this confession. 'Will you give me your undivided attention, Meg? Together we will make it work,' he said, skimming through my thesis proposal, his hands sleeping like two puppies on the table where ring marks from various coffee cups had created a kind of psychedelic pattern.

I was flattered that such a knowledgeable man, clearly on the fast track to academic glory would notice a red haired, freckled girl. At thirty, I had just about given up on the dating game and still lived with my mother in one of the pebble dashed cream townhouses in an estate just outside the university. My mother worked part-time as a librarian in the Science faculty and we often drove in together. I introduced her to Bill at one of the interdepartmental pre-Christmas social dos and later that night she told me, he had 'kind eyes. They're kind of droopy,' she said, nodding in approval. 'Meg, let's invite him home for tea. I'll bake him one of my cakes.'

My mother came from a long line of bakers. Her father had opened the first bakery in town after emigrating from Poland. His yeast poppy seed roll spun like a strudel was still talked about twenty years later. Victoria sponge, red velvet, Bundt marble and coffee cakes, my mother knew them all to her fingertips.

'Do you think it's appropriate to invite Bill home? I mean he's not exactly a friend. He's my supervisor. We aren't supposed to socialise?' I said to her.

'Of course, why wouldn't it be? He's similar in age and you are both involved in similar research. '

I invited Bill home the following weekend. 'I kind of wanted to see your set up,' he said. 'To see where those grey cells bloom at night.' He watched me intently as he said this and I felt a strange fuzzy kind of heat travel from the base of my spine to the top of my neck.

We sat in the kitchen and my mother smiled broadly as Bill ate his way through almost half of the walnut cake. 'It's exceedingly delicious. You must give me the recipe,' he kept saying, dabbing the side of his mouth with the blue linen napkin that my mother reserved for special occasions.

'Wait till you see her birthday cakes,' I said. My mother beamed with pride as I pulled out her baking album from one of the kitchen drawers. The album was covered in cellophane paper and each page had a picture of me standing next to a birthday cake. There I stood – aged two beside a pink teddy bear shaped birthday cake.

'Wow, just wow,' Bill kept saying, turning the pages where every milestone birthday was captured beside a suitably age-appropriate cake.

'Look at you, Meg at eighteen. Already quite a stunner,' Bill observed, his large thumb resting on my eighteen year old mouth. He lifted the album, bringing it closer to his face.

'Which rock band is it on the cake?' He turned to my mother who was looking over his shoulder, her steel-rimmed glasses pushed right up her nose.

'Oh, I was really into Duran Duran, those days, don't ask.' I giggled and closed the album.

'Yes, Duran Duran,' my mother said, her voice turning dreamy.

'It took me almost half a day to make those marzipan figurines and the guitar broke just as I was mounting it on the cake.'

'It's amazing how you managed to stay so slim, eating all that cake,' Bill said, grinning.

'Oh, we always gave it away,' I said. 'I was only ever allowed one slice.'

My mother nodded. 'It's an old Polish superstition. On

birthdays, you should never finish your own cake. We always gave it away.'

'Well, I can just imagine how fabulous Meg's wedding cake is going to be when she gets married,' Bill commented.

'Let's have some coffee,' I said putting away the album. 'We have herbal tea too if you want. Mint or verbena?'

'Why don't you show him the pergola in the garden,' my mother suggested after the coffee was finished and the plates cleared up and stored away.

'It's getting dark, Mum.' I looked out the window where the dark indigo night pressed itself against the glass panes.

'I'd love to take a look,' Bill said, springing up from his chair. Outside, the grass felt damp beneath our feet as we walked towards the wooden pergola.

'It's nothing special,' I told him. 'My father built it from scratch and he sculpted two Japanese cranes out of chicken wire and fixed them onto the trellis work. There they are.' I pointed out the two birds who were entwined in an awkward kind of embrace, their beaks pushed against each other and their thin, spindly legs tangled together.

'My father was very proud of his handiwork,' I finished rather lamely and shrugged. The birds looked plain and pathetic and I didn't know why I had brought Bill to see them.

'Well, aren't they beautiful! Such grace.' He pointed his mobile at them, lighting them up with the flash. 'Where's your father now?'

'Father died a couple of years back. He was a salesman for a carpet manufacturer, always on the road. I don't think he was ever there for a single birthday. He had a heart attack on one of those trips. Never came back.'

'Oh dear, I'm so sorry,' Bill lowered his voice and came closer. I felt his arm slowly go round my shoulder. He pulled me gently towards him. I felt his warm breath on the top of my head.

'My poor darling Meg. I'm going to make sure we celebrate your birthday every single year.' He turned me round and, lifting my chin with his index finger, he kissed me.

And I didn't push him away. I kissed him right back, pressing my fingernails into my palm, to steady the thumping of my heart.

We walked back to the house, our fingers lightly brushing each other's and my mother clapped her hands when she saw us.

'My instinct was right,' she told our friends a year later when we announced that we were getting married. 'I said to Meg, here's a man with a gooey soft marshmallow of a heart. He'll take proper care of you.'

*

My mother stayed up four nights putting the final touches to my three-tiered wedding cake topped with a pair of mint green doves made of champagne fondant holding a red strawberry heart. We took the cake with us on our honeymoon and Bill fed me a slice every night, just before we made love.

The years roll by. I give up on my PhD and we move towns. Three miscarriages and we give up on the idea of a family. I find a job at an actuarial company specialising in insolvency and Bill gets a fixed term tenure at the University. My mother visits us on my birthday and at Christmas. Her baking album slowly fills.

There's Bill on his fortieth, posing next to a cake designed to look like a medieval tower. My mother stands next to him, sparrow small, offering him a slice.

And just like that one Sunday in October, it's my turn. I became forty.

Bill is snoring gently when I nudge him. He turns, grunting, his morning breath sour and smelling of last night's dinner.

'Remember the date?' I say, shifting closer.

He yawns and rolls away, when all I want is for him to open wide the cave of his arms and for me to tiptoe in, his grizzly chin tickling the top of my head.

A little later, Bill is up, showered and ready in his Marks and Spencer blue checked shirt, the one with buttons on the collars and his green corduroy trousers with the crease in the centre. The steel buckle on his belt glints in the buttery autumn sunshine.

'I forgot to mention, but I'll be working late today.' Bill stands near the door, one hand gripping the handle, squinting towards me. His naked eyes look rabbit pink without his glasses.

'You don't teach on Sundays.' I keep my voice friendly.

'There are some extra classes I offered to teach. You know … what with exams next semester….the university wants us to step up. All this league table stuff…' His voice peters out. He swallows and his Adam's apple dances up and down.

Bill is still lecturing in medieval philosophy. He spends his days pontificating about the thinking of dead Greek and Italian men to bored students who would rather be in the cafeteria updating their Insta profiles while snacking on goji berries.

He sounds clever on his CV but his fixed term contract does

not do much to our bank account or his ego. He has to find ways to compensate.

'Well don't be late, honey.' My voice is candy floss. 'We're celebrating my birthday.' I try one more time.

'Of course it's your birthday…I've planned a little…' He hesitates and lets it pass, comes over and squeezes my arm. 'We'll go out for a special drink next week.' He throws me a crumb of a smile and shuts the door behind him.

I picture him in the kitchen opening the fridge, the cold blue light bathing his face as he grabs a slice of pepperoni pizza. He will eat it standing up, one large hand clumsily tapping love letters into his mobile. He will leave the coffee percolating for me. He is considerate like that but he will be gone on my fortieth birthday.

Gone to the Holiday Inn near the airport. The one with the faded flowery-carpeted corridors and plastic ferns pretending to be real. He'll occupy one of the rooms that sigh to the sound of lonely salesmen jerking off. There'll be a girl waiting inside a room. A slip of a girl probably from his first-year intake. She might be doing research in Machiavelli's war strategy. I could give her a tip or two. He will feed her chocolates and fairy tales about his unhappy marriage. She will look at him with wide, puppy soft eyes and let him unhook her lacy bra.

The only reason I know about the girl is that my best friend, Marge phoned me at work, her voice breathless with the juice of gossip she was about to spill.

'I don't want to upset you or anything…' she began. 'But I saw Bill at that fancy French restaurant, Chezz Pear. '

'Chay Pierre. The Z is silent,' I correct her. I have a B + in GCSE

15

French. My eyes stay fixed on the sea-blue computer screen where statistics tables of failing businesses roll down like ticker tape.

She continues. 'Bill was with a girl. I did wave to him, but he only had eyes for her. Cute little thing with a head of bouncy curls. There was a bottle of wine on the table and …' Her voice purrs with pleasure. 'They were holding hands. '

'Oh that girl?' I speed up. 'Yes, that must be Mabel. She's Special Needs. Needs one to one.'

'Are you sure? Does she need hand stroking too?'

'You're talking bullshit like always.' I hang up before she can destroy me more.

*

The first time Bill left the house on a weekend I followed him. He drove slowly, his grey Ford Mondeo waited patiently at the traffic lights. He drove towards the retail park and pulled up just outside the MacDonald's drive-through. A young girl came bounding out; she had blonde hair and a pile of books in her arms as alibi. Bill got out of the car and gave her a smacker on the mouth before opening the passenger door for her to slide in. I lost them at the second intersection but I knew where they were headed.

That evening I baked some gingerbread with cinnamon, ginger, cloves and cardamom, Bill's favourite.

'I'm not hungry,' Bill said when he came back home. He made a great show of placing his files and laptop on the kitchen table, flicking through the pages, his mouth pursed in concentration. 'I've had such a long day,' he added.

'But you're always hungry for my cake,' I said, pressing myself

16

against him so he could feel the excited hoofbeat of my heart. I pretend we are newlyweds again and unbuttoning my blouse, I guided his hand towards my breast.

'Meg, I'm not in the mood.' He pulled away.

*

My father had always been absent on my birthday, busy selling rolls of carpet to suburban housewives but my mum made sure the day was special. Bill knew that. He had also seen her baking album. Every birthday until I left home, she baked me a sponge cake, chocolatey and slushy, with a soft ganache centre that melted in my mouth. There was pink and blue icing and a silver flag shouting my name and candles brighter than Blackpool lights. The Queen would have envied such a cake. My mother would only let me eat one slice. 'One's enough. Don't be a greedy girl,' she said before packing the rest in shiny cellophane. We spent the rest of the evening driving around town hunting down drunken tramps and one-legged soldiers slumped in shopping arcades. My mother would nudge me towards them and say, 'Go share this cake and the love it holds. Go share it with those who need it most.' Afterwards we parked the car outside St. Ambrose Catholic Church and thanked the Lord for our blessings. When Bill first heard about our cake sharing excursions, he burst out laughing. 'But why even bother, sharing all that delicious cake. Are you some kind of Christian missionaries or what?' He tapped the side of his head and whispered, 'Cuckoo.' My mother and I had looked at each other. He was a man. You couldn't expect him to have understood.

*

Today on my fortieth birthday, with my mother dead and gone, I bake myself a birthday cake. I drive to Waitrose and load my trolley with organic flour, a dozen eggs and all the nutty, fruity trimmings to make the perfect cake. Rolling my sleeves, I set to work. I have my mother's recipe memorised back to front. Three hours later and the cake is ready in all its jiggly glory. Alternating layers of sponge and whipped cream, I spoon a thick layer of raspberry jam and a layer of custard, all topped with a coating of green marzipan once the cake is baked. Just before the cake is ready to go into the oven, I slip off my gold wedding band and place it right inside the wobbly heart of the cake.

I throw a tablecloth on the kitchen table, light the candelabra and wear my sequinned party frock. I crayon my lips in scarlet lipstick and tease my red hair into an artful mess. Sitting at the table, ready to feast, my mother's words come floating back. There's no need to be greedy. You must share this cake with those who need it most.

Gently I ease the cake into a box, tie it with a silver ribbon and drive across town to the hotel near the airport. It is easy to find him. Like most lecturers in medieval philosophy, Bill doesn't stray far from the truth. The room is booked under his own name. 'A special birthday delivery,' I assure the harassed receptionist who is fielding questions from a group of Americans brandishing maps. She waves me towards the lift.

I knock on the door of Room 215 and shout, 'Room service.' There is sunshine in my voice. A young girl wearing a towelling robe opens the door and sticks her head out. Her mascara has left footprints over her cheek and her curly hair is a tangle.

'Hello, young lady. I've got you some goodies,' I say.

'We didn't order anything,' she says in a high-pitched voice.

'Well, I think your boyfriend did.' It's easy enough to push her aside, she's feather light. I walk in, carrying my cake like a crown. The room stinks of second-rate love. There lies my husband, propped up against polyester pillows on the bed, his pale thighs and face flushed in post-coital bliss. His corduroy trousers are draped neatly on the back of a chair and the girl's lacy bra lies on top of his belt.

'What! Meg, what the hell are you doing here?' Bill shouts. His droopy eyes sink down further making him look like a cartoon. His hands rush down to pull up the beige checked duvet to cover his nakedness.

'Just thought I'd share my birthday cake with you. It's my fortieth and you, naughty boy, you forgot.' I tweak his cheek affectionately, just as my mother would. I place the cardboard box on the bedside table and bring out the cake. Bill's eyes move from the cake to my face, his mouth opens and shuts like a door but no sound comes out.

'Should I call security?' The girl whispers, reaching for the phone, but I'm quicker than her. I yank the telephone from its plug socket and fling it across the room.

'Sit down and don't say a word,' I tell her and she does just that, obedient little student that she is, she sits, watching me and wringing her hands.

Bill tries to get up but I push him down and whip aside his duvet, so he lies naked and defenceless like a newborn babe. Hitching up my dress, I clamber on top of him, sitting astride him, as though he's a horse, pinning him to the bed. I am intent on feeding Bill my cake. I lower my knee on his groin and keep his mouth open, my fingers wedged tight against his palette. He is sputtering something. His eyes are watering. One slice, then two, and then a third. I feed him quietly with my free hand. He's making clown faces at me now, round-eyed in fear, his mouth jammed with cake. Green icing dribbles from the side of his mouth. The girl stands by the side of the bed, sobbing. 'Please stop, please stop,' she repeats again and again. She looks needy and hungry. I feed her some cake too. There are even leftovers that I take home.

Later that night, after showering and getting ready for bed, I go downstairs for one last slice. I notice that my wedding band is missing in the leftovers. I don't really care. I am satiated and complete – the warm feel of my birthday cake snug in my husband's belly.

*

Meg Kowalski's birthday cake
Ingredients
Three layer cake bases.
One portion pastry cream around 600g.
600 ml whipping cream.
2 tbsp. icing sugar.
150 g raspberry jam.
200 g green marzipan lid.
Pink and green modelling icing for flowers and leaves decorations.
Piping bag, spatula, cake stand.
Wedding ring-optional.

STRANGER IN THE MIRROR

Nadia Kabir Barb

The photograph on the table showed a slender young woman in a blue floral shirt and jeans gazing up at the man next to her, a smile on her lips. The man was laughing, his head tilted back, arm resting on her shoulder. There was something intimate about the way she was looking at him. I felt like a voyeur, an intruder. The woman, my mother, looked carefree, vibrant and most importantly, happy. An emotion I had seen only in bursts and flashes. I remembered a woman whose smile didn't quite reach her eyes, a sadness in them I had never entirely understood. I placed the photo face down on the table and rubbed my temple. The image of the two of them was seared into my brain.

There was an inscription on the back written in a bold hand though the ink had faded over time. 'Always yours, Adam'. The man in the picture wasn't my father. He was a curly-haired man with dark eyebrows over smiling, hazel eyes. If I hadn't gone into my parents' bedroom after the funeral, I would never have found the photograph. It had slipped from my hand, the back of the frame coming loose when it fell on the floor. The photograph had been tucked inside.

It was strange to think that more than six weeks had passed since the accident.

When I arrived at the hospital, the woman at the reception had directed me where to go. The doctor who spoke to me had the careworn face of someone who had seen too much pain and suffering. He informed me that a lorry had skidded on the motorway and ploughed into their car. My mother had been killed instantly by the impact and my father hadn't regained consciousness after the crash. 'I'm very sorry for your loss, Mr Rasheed…' The information had been imparted with just the right balance of sympathy and calm. It was clearly not the first time he had given this kind of speech. My legs buckled. The doctor steadied me and led me to a chair.

DOA. Dead on arrival. And with those three words I was an orphan. Arguably 'orphan' was a term that could no longer be applied to me. After a certain age you cease to be an orphan and become 'parentless'. At the age of twenty-four, however, orphaned is exactly how I felt. Losing both parents at the same time was something I never imagined I would have to confront. Identifying them was a cold and impersonal process, incongruous with how I felt. The sight of their lifeless bodies is an image I will never be able to erase. For days, I walked around in a fog, my brain numb.

I'm not sure I could have dealt with the situation if it wasn't for Zia Chacha, my father's younger brother. As soon as he heard the news, he packed his bags and his family into their battered but dependable Volkswagen Passat and drove down from Birmingham. My Dadi, Dad's mother, had died when he was still in school and my Dada passed away a couple years ago. Since then, it had just been the two of them.

'Don't worry about a thing, Amer,' he said as he embraced me, patting me awkwardly on the back. Displays of physical affection made him uncomfortable, reminding me of Dad. 'I'll sort out the funeral and burial arrangements.'

I could only nod in thanks. At the time, I didn't even stop to think how hard it was for him having just lost his brother.

The janazah service took place at the local mosque and never having been particularly devout I was at a loss as to what the formalities and rituals were. Neither of my parents had been particularly observant either. I had only attended a couple of janazahs when friends of Mum and Dad had died but had just copied everyone else at the mosque. Afterwards I told Mum it was a bit like playing 'Simon Says', only in this case it was 'The Imam Says'. I remember her trying hard not to laugh and telling me off half-heartedly for my irreverence.

I had abdicated responsibility without a moment's hesitation and was ashamed of how relieved I had been accepting my uncle's offer to shoulder the burden. Saira Chachi, his equally efficient wife, had taken charge of looking after all the people who came to pay their respects and for a while the house had hummed with life.

The funeral had taken place straight after the janazah. We gathered on a crisp autumn day, the sun bathing the mourners in its golden light as we put my parents to rest. The finality of the situation hit me only when we lowered Mum and Dad into their graves, both bodies wrapped in white cotton shrouds. With each fistful of soil, it was as if the air in my lungs was being squeezed out.

A horn blaring outside made me start. I don't know how long I had been sitting in the kitchen, immersed in my thoughts, chasing a carousel of unanswered questions. The sun had gone down. The only light in the room was borrowed from the streetlamps. A still life photograph in sepia I thought, looking around the room. Everything was just as it had always been. The same old white plastic clock that Dad had picked up from Woolworths years ago over the door; the limestone tiles chosen with care when they had renovated the house; the motley collection of mugs my mother had accumulated over the years. Frozen in time, immortalising the past.

My fingers traced the initials carved into the wooden kitchen table – a show of teenage rebellion. 'I didn't bring you up to be a vandal! It's that bloody Pete from next door that's making you behave like this.' I heard this frequently from Dad when I did something he didn't approve of. He would replace the word 'vandal' with 'lout', 'ingrate' or anything befitting my perceived misdemeanour. Poor Pete, my neighbour and childhood friend, took an inordinate amount of flak. 'That's what mates do,' he would say and add that my Mum's cooking was reward enough for putting up with it. He was living on the Gold Coast now, a surfing instructor with his Aussie girlfriend. We spoke briefly after he heard the news of my parents. I wish he were here; his pragmatic advice would have been welcome. But the photo didn't feel like a topic you could discuss over the phone.

I needed a caffeine boost. The cupboard held an impressive assortment of teas with a lonely jar of instant coffee hiding right at the back, like an afterthought. Both my parents had a penchant for tea. I took out the mug which said, 'Keep calm and drink tea'. It seemed appropriate. The fridge had been emptied but there was a carton of milk lurking inside. I sniffed it and gagged. It came out in clumps as I poured it down the sink, a rancid smell filling the air.

The kitchen was silent except for the ticking of the clock. The silence was unfamiliar. I could still hear the echoes of my parents' raised voices, arguing about something, everything and nothing. Thrust and parry, they were experts at fencing with words. It was like watching the same show on loop, ending only when Dad would slam the door behind him and retreat into the living room to drink himself into oblivion. Mum would sit at the table, her face blotchy from crying. 'You're such a good son, I don't deserve you,' she would say as I made her a cup of tea and waited for the tears to subside.

Later, I would find Dad asleep on the sofa, his glass lying on the floor beside him and a whiskey bottle on the table. I lost count of the number of times we enacted the scene where I would help him upstairs, finally getting him into bed after taking his shoes off. Picking up the marital pieces was a burden my parents had thoughtlessly deposited on my teenage shoulders and I had resented them for it.

University had been my escape, a route to freedom, and I gladly accepted the offer from Edinburgh, getting as far away as I could. I never moved back home. A job in the City beckoned and I jumped at the opportunity. Mum said I didn't come home often enough, but somehow life just got in the way. Now they were both gone. All I was left with was a room full of ghosts. Right now, I would have done anything to see their faces and hear their voices. There were times in the past few weeks I had called the home phone letting it ring till it went to voicemail just to listen to the recorded message. I wondered whether I would ever get used to the pain that had taken up permanent residency inside my chest.

'Always yours, Adam.' I read the words out loud. I could feel the tension building in my shoulders. I picked up the photograph, walked into the hallway and switched the light on in the downstairs toilet.

I held up the photo and scrutinised it against the reflection in the mirror. The mouth and shape of face were different. My face was longer and more angular while the man in the photo had a wider face with a square jaw. But the deep-set hazel eyes were similar to my own, down to the straight brows hanging over them. And the hair was unruly like my own. I had never paid any attention to how little I resembled my Dad nor had I wondered why. It's not something you think about. People said I looked like Mum; she was fair like a lot of Sylhetis. I thought I had inherited my colouring from her. Dad was of medium build and height, with a rapidly receding hairline. His face was round and more heavily set. Towering over both my parents at 6'2", I just thought I had got lucky and missed out on their 'short' genes.

When Lily had first seen the photo, she asked if it was a relative of mine, 'Who's that? Another one of your relations? He looks like you.' The comment had somehow taken root in my mind.

The harsh sound of the doorbell was a much-needed reprieve from my thoughts. I took a deep breath and walked back into the hallway. There was only one person I was in the mood to see. Lily's smiling face greeted me as I opened the door. She hugged me, standing on her toes to kiss me. I enveloped her in my arms and buried my face in her long dark hair, drinking in the sweet smell of her perfume.

'How're you feeling?'

I shook my head wordlessly as I released her and shut the door behind us.

The kitchen was dark, and she switched the lights on. It brought me back to the stark reality of the present, banishing the ghosts of the past.

'What's that awful smell?' She wrinkled her nose in distaste.

'Sorry, forgot to throw the milk away last time...,' I trailed off.

The photograph was still in my hand and she reached out and took it from me.

'Did you find anything else?'

'Haven't actually looked.'

'Why don't we order some food, then start with the photos? You never know. We might find something,' said Lily, already reaching for her mobile phone.

I don't know what I had done to deserve Lily, but I was grateful for her presence in my life. We had met on a train going up to Newcastle, sitting next to each other, and started up a conversation. A year later and here we were. She was my lifeline, keeping me sane while my world slowly crumbled around me.

Once the pizzas had been eaten and the boxes cleared away, we went upstairs. Over the years the guest bedroom had served a dual-purpose, housing visitors and an assortment of books, albums and boxes of unidentified objects, in fact anything that had no place in my parents' day-to-day life.

We sat on the floor, each of us with a pile of photo albums and loose photographs we had found stored in one of the boxes. It was a strange feeling flipping through the pages, seeing Mum and Dad gazing back at me. I'm not sure what I expected to find but I needed to do something.

We sat in silence as we sifted through the photos.

'Good God is this you?' said Lily holding up a picture of a young boy with a fake moustache and painted beard.

'I'd forgotten about that. I was one of the wise men in the school nativity play. Must have been five.'

My parents were kneeling beside me, their faces filled with pride. I remembered how pleased they had been with me for getting a 'starring role' in the play. I flicked through snapshots of sports days with Dad, playing on the beach in Spain, ice-creams in Brighton, Mum sitting in the kitchen, the sunlight catching her face as she smiled down at me but none of the photographs elicited anything other than a deep sense of nostalgia. With each album and each photograph, memories that had been relegated to the deep recesses of my mind began to resurface.

'I don't think there's anything here,' I felt weary and defeated. Lily nodded in agreement.

'I'm trying to think when all this changed,' I said pointing to the photographs. 'Do you think it was because of him?'

'I don't know. Maybe,' said Lily, wrapping her arms around me. 'He was probably just an ex-boyfriend.'

'I wonder why Mum hid the photo and why she never mentioned him. It's not like we didn't talk about stuff.'

Lily disentangled herself and started putting the albums and photographs back in their boxes. 'Look it's getting late. We're seeing Katherine tomorrow. Hopefully, she'll know something.' I hoped she was right.

I took her hand and led her to the room next door – my old bedroom. The Star Wars poster hung above my bed, my guitar still on its stand in the corner of the room. They had left it untouched. Later, I lay on the bed, Lily's head on my shoulder, looking up at the ceiling. The last thing I remember before sleep claimed me was the image of Mum and Adam smiling.

*

Lily and I sat on a small red sofa in Katherine's flat in North Harrow waiting for her to say something. Katherine was Mum's best friend from her days as a student and the two had always been close. Katherine had been a constant during my life, her presence solid and reassuring. I watched her face intently for any sign of recognition or emotion. She looked up from the photograph.

'Jesus, this is a blast from the past! I do remember him. God, this was way back... when your mum and I were still in uni. I've forgotten where Roxy met him but they...' Katherine stopped and stared at the mug of Earl Grey tea in her hands. She was one of the few people who called Mum 'Roxy', shortened from Roksana.

'They what?' I could feel my body tensing like a steel coil wound too tight. Lily reached out and squeezed my hand.

'They were inseparable, even though he was studying in UCL. No hang on, it was King's College I think. He'd come and spend time whenever he could. At one point they even talked about getting married.' The look on her face made me realise that the loss of my mother, her best friend, was not inconsiderable.

'So he was an old boyfriend.'

'What happened?' asked Lily.

Katherine put her mug down, 'I just know that during the

29

summer holidays in our…second year, it must have been, she called me saying she was getting married to your Dad after she graduated. I don't think she had a choice. Sorry to say this but your grandad was a bloody tyrant!' There was a flash of anger in her eyes. 'They found out about Adam… and God forbid a love marriage. I think Adam took it really hard—.'

'Mum just married Dad because she had to? They told me it was arranged, families knew each other…'

'Your grandad wouldn't let her finish her studies unless she agreed to the marriage.'

'Crikey, he sounds hideous, Amer,' said Lily, raising her hands in the air.

I didn't disagree. The last time I had seen Nana a few years back, I had to stop myself from telling him he was an ignorant, opinionated bigot – a living anachronism. Thank God he had moved back to Bangladesh when I was just a kid.

'All I know is that your mum and Adam stopped seeing each other after that,' said Katherine. 'Though she told me she did meet Adam again a few years later but that's all I know.'

'Before I was born?'

Katherine nodded. Mum had seen Adam while she was married to Dad. I sat down and ran my fingers through my hair. I tried to think back, searching for any significant signs of what might have happened. Had Dad started drinking because he found out about Mum and Adam, the ex-boyfriend, maybe an ex-lover – the thought was like a punch in the gut. Were my parents really ever happy together? I knew that it was an arranged marriage. Mum and her family lived in London and Dad had grown up in Birmingham. Right after she had graduated, my grandfather had fixed her marriage with Dad. The families had known each other for years. Mum had let slip a long time ago that my grandfather didn't approve of the friends she had made at university. I wondered if she was referring to Adam. They both looked pretty young in the photograph. Where was he now? The more I asked myself these questions, the less I realised I knew. My parents were becoming strangers to me.

'She really tried to make a go of it with your Dad but ultimately they just weren't the right fit.'

'Did you take the photo?'

'I can't remember. I might have.' Katherine said uncertainly.

Obviously, my parents had a past but the thought I had been trying to bury surfaced again. 'Can I ask you a question?'

'Yes, of course.'

'Do you see any similarities with...Adam and me?' I said holding up the picture.

She looked at the picture and then at me. 'I...well, there might be but... I mean now you mention it...,' her hands rested on her lap as she twirled the ring around her finger. I could see Katherine struggling to accept that her best friend for decades may have kept secrets from her as well. Betrayal wasn't as exclusive as I had thought.

People lie. It's a fact of life and no matter how we dress it up, a lie by any other name is still a lie. Sometimes we pretend we're protecting a loved one, but if we're honest, we do it mostly to protect ourselves. Sometimes, silence is easier than confronting the truth. I guess my parents were no different.

'You know it might not be what you're thinking, Amer. She never told me. I'm not saying you're wrong, I just don't know,' said Katherine with a shake of her head.

'Right now, this is all conjecture,' Lily added, 'You don't know the full story. Seriously, if I said you look like some movie star it doesn't mean he's your brother or your father. All we're doing is just jumping to a whole load of conclusions. It might—'

'I know,' I said, cutting Lily off. 'But what if it is true. Katherine said Mum met up with him after she was married to Dad.'

'You could do a DNA test…,' she said looking expectantly at me.

'What, you mean exhume their bodies and get a sample of hair or saliva, yeah sure, why not.'

'Toothbrush, hairbrush…' Lily trailed off as I turned to look at her.

'This isn't a fucking crime drama.' I knew I was being unnecessarily harsh but the words were out before I could stop myself.

Katherine smoothed her short blonde hair as she stood up, 'Give me a sec, I had an address for him or his parents, can't remember which but it's from years ago.'

'Look sorry babe, I didn't…' I said as Katherine left the room. Lily raised her hand and stopped me before I could finish. She said nothing as we waited, and I was grateful for the silence. The noise in my head was deafening.

After about five minutes, Katherine came back with a black and white floral notebook in hand.

'Thank God we used to actually write things down in our day.' She sat back in the armchair opposite the sofa and flicked through the pages.

'Adam,' she said, a look of triumph on her face.

I felt as if the air had been sucked out of the room. For a moment it was hard to breathe. I took the diary she handed to me. His name was Lucas Adam.

As if reading my mind, Lily said, 'Wonder why on earth he used his last name if his name is Lucas.'

'Not sure, actually,' replied Katherine, her face creasing into a frown. 'We all called him Adam.'

'Thank you, Katherine, I really appreciate—'

'I wish I could do more. I wish I knew more. Amer, he probably doesn't live there anymore but I hope it's a start.'

I wondered how many Lucas Adams there were in the world. But at least I had a name and an address. It was definitely a start.

'So, what do you want to do?' said Lily, pulling the cushion against her chest.

'I don't know,' I said, handing the diary back to Katherine. What I did know was finding Lucas Adam would be the only way to make sense of what the photo signified. Acknowledging that something might be true was one thing, knowing that it was true, another. But accepting the truth… I wasn't sure I could deal with that. At least, not for now.

THE UNUSUAL PROPERTIES OF CORK

Kavita A. Jindal

Despite what people say about me and the life I led, it wasn't that often that I travelled distances just to have a special meal. In those days there were many people who took pride in being foodies and in straying afar for a special event.

I did go to north Sweden for a much-hyped dinner which wasn't even for a special celebration. Afonso Mello had asked me to accompany him. He was the guy I had a smoothie with after our gym sessions. We attended the same core workout and then we took our aching butts to the lounge and rested. We had the same bored exercise style. We needed to be kicked and then we treated ourselves to self-care.

The woman Afonso was dating had just broken up with him. He seemed more distraught about the cancellation of an extraordinary and exceptional meal than the disastrous end of his relationship. He'd booked Faviken restaurant six months previously and didn't want to cancel and didn't want to go alone. That's how it happened, and don't tell me that life is predictable.

So many things can only be explained in hindsight. In the moment, you just live.

Afonso was a friend, but I'd never had dinner with him. I don't think I was his type of woman. But I didn't know that sort of thing about him and he certainly didn't know that sort of thing about me. He did ask nicely if I would accompany him. 'Chef Magnus Nilsson', he said, eyes shining at the prospect, as if I would know. I looked it up on duckduckgo (not google) and saw what a treat it would be. Summer in the Scandinavian countryside, locally grown and hunted ingredients. I had nothing planned for the weekend Afonso had mentioned. A walk by the river. A long walk by the river, singing, if no one was within earshot. But hey, I was footloose and fancy free, and when I checked the plane ticket availability and prices, I was happy to give it a shot. That's how I went from London to Sweden one summer weekend.

We arrived at Faviken, in the transcendent light of a Nordic evening, having driven for six hours from Stockholm, talking about the scenery en route and guessing what would be on the menu for dinner. We were shown to our rustic room which Afonso had chosen when he'd booked. He didn't want to be driving or taxiing to a nearby town after his 'wine-matched' feasting. There were only a handful of rooms in the restaurant's own lodgings and they were all the same: two single beds, each hugging a wall, and a furry rug on the floor between. The ends of our beds hit the small window, round like a porthole, from which we could spy on the path leading to the restaurant. Our fellow diners were already heading to the restaurant patio to gather for drinks. We'd been given the time of 7 p.m. to assemble. Dinner service would start then.

We took turns to dress for dinner. Afonso went on ahead, European smart-casual, pale colours, and looking just right. I got in a muddle deciding what to do with my messy hair and so arrived a bit late. I'd settled for a low ponytail tied with a green crushed-velvet scrunchie. My dress was black splashed with yellow irises.

As I stepped onto the verandah, staff began ushering guests into the dining room. They'd been waiting for me. I got the impression that the restaurant ran to a strict schedule. That impression settled into confirmation as the evening wore on. We diners may have been paying big money for a world-famous restaurant and fancyschmancy dishes but we were being treated a bit like schoolchildren. No deviating from what we were expected to do, which, funnily enough, was to follow firm orders. Afonso and the other diners didn't seem to mind, but I found it amusing. I enjoyed disregarding the head waiter's pronouncements. Just occasionally, but enough to irk him.

It also irked Afonso which wasn't my intention. But then it was probably not Afonso's intention to bore me, but he did. Not with the food, or the magnificent wines, or the restaurant itself, or the whole experience, but with his courteous insistence on answering my silly question: what are you passionate about?

Cork.

He answered so fully between courses, of which there were thirteen, that I had plenty of time to overdrink while I listened. Cork. His family in Portugal farmed it. For generations. I can tell you a lot about cork. It's up to you how much to believe of what I say. It is indestructible, did you know? It is vegan, yes. You can send it to the moon and aliens will return it to us one day.

Before each course the head waiter clapped his hands so that we could fall silent to hear his pronouncement about the course to be served along with instructions about how to consume it. Which spoon or fork. All in one go or not. Use hands or not. Eat the side with it, after it, before it, or not! I joke not. He told us what we would taste, what we would feel. There was no menu to read and so we had to listen very carefully to what he said. I hissed, 'What, what?' when I heard 'Veal, colt's foot' and 'Colostrum with meadowsweet' and my companion said, 'Shh' and the waitress at our table, gently pouring my wine, admonished, 'No talking just now.' Later I realised how clever this show was. How we strained to hear and pay attention with all our senses. The following day, when we left, we were given the menu but at the time of the announcements, I couldn't really be sure what I was hearing. 'What? what?' I said to Afonso when I heard 'Lupin curd gratin' and 'Mahogany clam with beer vinegar' and 'A small egg coated in ash, sauce made from dried trout and pickled marigold'. 'Shh' Afonso said.

Early on I gave up on what I was meant to do and poked my fork rudely into my scallop, "skalet ur elden" cooked over burning juniper branches. I concentrated on the wines that enchantingly appeared at each course. 'Goodness, Afonso,' I said, between euphoric sips, 'thank you for this, it's *amazing*' and then I said, 'Tell me more about cork, Afonso.'

I'm not sure if I was being flippant, but he took me at face-value, which was good of him, and poured out his heart. He missed Portugal and would return there, he said, to his family's bosom when he was done with London. He would grow old harvesting the trees that he planted since it took twenty-five years for them to yield. Cork oaks can be harvested every nine years once they're mature. The year of harvest is marked on the trunk so trees don't get harvested by mistake at the wrong time. Cork is a sustainable substance, of course it is! Premium wine corks last fifty years. Fifty. Who keeps wine that long? Well, Afonso's family do.

By dessert, diners were talking across tables to each other, especially the Italian group on one side of us who winked and sang and threw questions at us, and then the men made mortified faces like naughty schoolboys when the head-waiter clapped at them. Their ladies giggled and after the next course had been duly proclaimed, they stage-whispered to me that they were there celebrating a host of events: anniversaries, birthdays, promotions.

I felt Afonso grow a bit sad as I got merry with them. There were six delicious dessert courses, in tiny portions, as if we humans were fragile, earth-loving creatures who didn't over-consume. As if these little bites were what we ate and not five hundred grams of lemon drizzle cake in one sitting. I only talk about me of course. What do I know of the others? From my keepsake menu I can tell you what was served for the sweet end of dinner:

Rhubarb baked in pearl sugar, very fresh cottage cheese
Raspberry Ice
Bone marrow pudding; frozen milk; pickled semi-dried root vegetables
Meat and birch pie
A selection of tar pastilles, meadowsweet candy, dried rowan berries, smoked caramel, sunflower seed nougat, dried blackcurrant
Aromatic seeds; Snus fermented in a used bitters barrel.

That last one was snuff, and I went for it. Afonso delicately declined.

When dinner was over and we were allowed to file out into the wondrous light of night, Afonso settled on the patio with a French couple. They were both doctors and their conversation veered towards the rise and rise of curcumin. Afonso was enthusiastic. Perhaps he could discuss anything at length. I broke in, somewhat nonchalantly, 'Yes, I know all about it. Curcumin is an active ingredient in turmeric. In Ayurveda, turmeric has been prescribed for its anti-inflammatory and immune-boosting properties for generations. In fact, in Ayurveda, the ancient Indian medicine system which you must have heard of', I gestured to the two physicians, 'we've known about curcumin for five thousand years.'

I clicked my fingers and left them on the veranda. I went into the tepee set up on flat ground opposite. There was a fire burning inside, in the middle. Round benches followed the circle of the tepee and I was beckoned to a cushioned seat by the Italian group who were merrily ensconced in there. Their celebrations continued apace as we smoked cigars and knocked back cognacs. Afonso came looking for me at 3 a.m. and in that duskiest hour of the night, we straggled back to our room. I fell into my bed. But too much wine makes me an unruly sleeper, and after I'd wriggled on one side and then the other, I turned towards the other bed and saw that Afonso was wide awake.

'Oh Afonso, am I a terrible date?'

'No,' he said. He held out his hand across the rug. 'Hold my hand.'

I did. It seemed to soothe him. 'Oh Afonso,' I asked again. 'Do you want to sit up and chat?' I didn't add, 'And not about the properties of cork trees.'

'Sort of,' he replied. He seemed rather forlorn and I felt that perhaps I had let him down. I went across to him and told him how incredible the experience had been.

'I know,' he said. 'I knew it would be worthwhile.' His chin went up towards the porthole. 'Look at that sky.' He settled his head on to my shoulder and went to sleep in a few minutes, his snores soft and child-like.

I thought I'd had a glimpse into his soul as I listened to his deep sighing breaths and watched the light outside return to a crisp brightness as it became morning and time for breakfast. Yet more food. Afonso appeared rested but even though I'd scrubbed my face twice and splashed cold water on it, I felt completely groggy. Afonso took my hand as we walked the path to the breakfast terrace, he held my hand on the flight home, and that's when I knew we would remain friends for a very long time because when Afonso took my hand on that trip he smiled and he was happy, and his extrovert happiness made me laugh. I didn't say it, but I also cherished his generous spirit, although aloud I made fun of most of what he had to say.

On the flight back Afonso told me he kept his friends for fifty years.

My jokey response to that would come much later. Afonso would, true to his word, call regularly for a chat – he did like to talk – even after he returned to Portugal and had a family and little ones. Fifty years wouldn't pass for Afonso. When he was certain he was dying and had told his friends, I became the one who phoned regularly and who talked more than him, to save him the labour of speech. One of the things I said to him before he died: 'People from India keep their friends for five thousand years. Remember, Afonso? Go laughing, and take some cork with you.'

MY BABY'S EYES

Mona Dash

I am in a panic. The parking bays are full and the only available space is between two cars. It means I will have to attempt a parallel park. I try, drive alongside the first car, reverse the way I have been taught to, but it doesn't work, and I almost graze the shiny black Audi in front. Then I try to come in at an angle, drive in and straighten up deftly, but the back of my car sticks out. Maybe I should give up and ask Nick to buy the paints over the weekend but I can't cope with his face when he hears I wasn't able to parallel park yet again! I drive around and look for another space, nothing, and here I am, back to where I started. Except that there is now a white delivery van expertly parked.

The driver of the van steps out, a tall guy, smiling. At me? Has he seen my pathetic attempts to park? Like so many others, like my driving instructor who would sit there shaking his head, 'I don't understand this, you teach in the college, you must be clever, right? And yet, you aren't able to do a manoeuvre?' And Nick, his face contorted, patience running dry, his voice snapping, 'Steer to the left, left, left! For God's sake, Uma, don't you know your left from your right?' Sunday afternoon and he would be giving me parking lessons in the local Tesco car park. Bay parking, parallel parking; my hands trembling, my brain turning soft. Sometimes I wonder if I am on the dyspraxia spectrum.

I catch the driver's eye, and suddenly, he is alongside me.

'Yes?' I roll down my window.

'You alright?'

'Yes. I am…' my voice on edge, why wouldn't I be?

'Well, I mean,' he shrugs, gesturing at my car, then at the space around. That's when I realise I am in the way, blocking any vehicle that might come in or want to leave. He wears a white t-shirt and jeans. A dimple flashes on his left cheek. Something about his eyes. So honest, so open.

'There's no space to park. Maybe if I wait long enough someone will leave,' I explain.

'Look, Miss, there's one, right there.' Indeed there is. Another tiny spot between two massive SUVs.

'That's not going to work.' He looks at me with such a look of surprise that I blurt, 'Well I can't manoeuvre into that space. I just can't.'

'I see,' shrugging again, he walks away. Then suddenly, he looks back. His hair falls over his forehead. And I smile broadly thinking how nice he looks.

'Would you like me to help?'

There's nothing to lose. 'Yes, please, will you?' I get out of the car, wondering if he meant he would guide me or park my car. With a quick shrug, he gets in, pushes the seat to accommodate his longer legs and reverses.

I relax. It is a beautiful day in spring, the daffodils and snowdrops are out. The magnolia in my garden is in full bloom. On days like this, when everything feels alive, I can believe it will happen, that I can pat my life into a perfect ever-after.

And he is next to me, handing me the keys.

'Thank you so much! I am Uma, by the way.'

'My pleasure, Ooma. I am Charlie.'

'Not often that this happens! I can park my car...well, usually.'

'That's OK,' his eyes take up the smile after it leaves his mouth.

'Actually, I am a new driver but I can't park to save my life!' I don't know why I tell him this but my frustration at myself spills out before I can stop it.

'I see. ' He stands there, in the sun, looking at the P plates on my Mini Cooper. He stands there looking at me, I mean, really looking at me.

'You work here?' I know I am stalling. I am suddenly curious about him, such a helpful young man, so courteous. I imagined delivery van drivers were middle-aged, rough, prone to speeding.

'I do a delivery to Carpet Right, a few times in the week. And you?'

'I am at Reading University.'

'Studying there?'

'You flatter me! I teach.'

'What do you teach?'

'Physics.'

He whistles, 'Wow, you are clever!'

'You really flatter me! Thanks again. I need to go, need to get some stuff, in a bit of a rush.'

'And I need to get the carpets out. Get on to the next job.'

43

I feel his eyes on me as I walk to the home decor shop. I look back and wave. He waves back.

That evening I think of him. When I tell Nick I have bought the paints, I don't mention my parking debacle.

Two days later, my period arrives, unfailing like the sun in its duty to rise. It's during my first class for the day. I just know. I know that feeling now. I rush to the bathroom and see it, a thick smudge of blood, staining the beige knickers.

Later, I call Nick. He knows, just from my voice. 'Don't worry darling, next time,' he says, calm as always.

I can't remain unperturbed. Something isn't working and it isn't under my control. Change myself, turn my body inside out, coat it with something, trap the sperm, conceive, conceive, conceive, but it seems my insides are dead. Fertile thoughts are of no help. We have been trying for three years. We've both had tests; nothing wrong with either of us. The doctors' diagnosis is almost an oxymoron: unexplained infertility. Some clomid cycles, to no avail, and then a cancelled IVF cycle last year. I am a poor responder and don't produce enough follicles. It happens at times, they say. Unlucky. They advise us to try naturally for a while, after all, there is no identifiable problem, but if we aren't successful and want to try a cycle again, we can come back and they will try a different drug on me. As every month comes and goes, I feel the desperation rise and permeate my very cells. The longing grows like winter shadows.

I am restless. I will go home. When Nick arrives, we will have dinner, we will watch some TV, we will calmly chart the cycle, make a note of the fertile dates on the calendar in the kitchen.

I will go to bed first. He will come later. We will feel thankful there's no sex tonight, no pressure on us, but we won't mention this to each other. I do know Nick isn't as desperate as I am to become a parent. 'Uma, many couples don't have children,' he says often. But I feel trapped in my body, helpless, and everything outside seems solid-still and unchanging.

The next day, I feel an urge to break the day itself, as if shattering china. I drive to the retail park during my lunch hour. A few times a week he had said. Didn't that mean every other day? I am right. The familiar white van is there! I even find an empty bay, not too far from the van, and drive into it. Charlie walks out of the store, a few minutes later.

'Hey,' I say, rolling down my window, as if I have just noticed him.

'Huh? Hello?' Then he recognises me. 'Oh, the clever Professor!"

'You've forgotten my name!'

'Not at all. Ooma, how are you?'

I have an odd desire to rumple his curls, he looks so young. 'I'm fine. How about you?' I step out of the car. 'I wanted to practise my driving. Decided to come up since it's lunch break and grab a sandwich. What a surprise to run into you!'

'Ah OK.' Maybe I didn't have to explain. He doesn't seem very surprised, nor does he seem in a hurry, so out of the blue, it comes out, 'I'm going to the Costa opposite. Want to join me?'

If he thinks it's an odd suggestion, he doesn't show it. 'Why not? I have some time before the next delivery so...yes..' We cross the road and head to the other part of the retail park. We

45

find a table at the far end. I insist on buying. A ham and cheese toastie, a Coke, a tuna melt, orange juice.

'So, practising driving…why?' He asks.

'Just to build my confidence, you know? Be able to park efficiently, get on the motorway. I passed my test some months ago after five attempts!'

'Five? Expensive. Looks like they were tough on you!'

'No, I mess up, really mess up.' I describe my various manoeuvring horrors. How I'd ended up on the other side of the road when trying to reverse the corner, and the examiner said, 'This is interesting.' How I'd ended up a metre from the kerb when I tried to parallel park and stalled in the attempt.

'Drive an automatic then, it's easier.'

'My husband said the best way to learn to drive is in a manual car.' Nick knew everything about cars. It hadn't occurred to me to disagree with him.

'Hmmm.. OK. You've been married long?'

'Ten years.' Suddenly it feels tedious. Ten whole years. 'And you?'

'I have a girlfriend…but she's gone back to Cape Town to her parents. Told me today she doesn't know if she will come back. Wants to go to college, you see…'

'She could go to college here, isn't it?'

'I don't know…she sort of left,' he looks worried, so I change the topic.

'And you? Where did you study?'

He blushes red. He confesses he dropped out of school. He is good with his hands, that's about all. Sometimes he dreams of studying, maybe part-time. But he doesn't even know what he should study, he doesn't know enough about the courses offered.

'Oh I can help you there! Why don't you come to the next open day we have at the university? They have several programs to help youth get back into education.'

'Youth! Me?'

'Of course.! You are so young.'

'Not that young. I am twenty-five. Too late for me.'

'You have all the time! Only twenty-five.' I laugh outright. I was already married by the time he was in his teens. Nick was a senior business consultant. I was a junior lecturer. We'd bought a little flat overlooking the river. We had made plans to move out in a few years, buy a semi with a garden, have three kids. We'd assumed all that we dreamt would be realised. All this before Charlie had his first kiss perhaps.

As if reading my thoughts, he asks, 'And you have kids, yes?'

When he says the word, his brown eyes large, his eyelashes inordinately long, his face so kind, so young, I feel tears well up. I feel that smudge of blood between my legs. I hear the voices chanting in my head, *poor responder, infertility, unlucky, not in your hands, keep trying…* And now the tears are spilling like water from an overfull glass. How silly to cry before a stranger. But he seems so easy to trust, so nice. I seem to be doing a lot of things I don't usually do.

'I'm so sorry,' he says, 'I didn't mean to upset you.' He reaches over the small table and holds my hand. His palms are rough on my manicured hand.

'It's not your fault. It's…it's just that we can't have kids.'

Finally it is out in the open. Like the sun on a hot day exposing every little nook. The little truth Nick and I hadn't said even to ourselves. The fact that we may never become parents.

'And I can't even park properly,' I am sobbing now.

'But what's that got to do with babies?' Charlie looks perplexed.

'It's all me, hopeless, a failure, can't respond properly, can't do anything right.'

He stands up and comes across, bends, gives me a hug, all warm arms and dimples. 'I am sorry about the baby but if you want, I can help you with the driving and parking!'

'I am so bad that my driving instructor was happy to say goodbye to me.'

'That's rich of him, considering you were paying him! Try this one, free.'

'Quid Pro Quo. We will sort out a nice course for you.'

So that's how it starts. We meet in my lunch break on the days he is free. He watches me as I drive, he gives me advice about manoeuvring, his voice steady. My car changes from a cumbersome, impulsive thing to something under my control. Having grown up with chauffeurs in India, then years without a car in London, I had never needed to be behind a wheel. Charlie on the other hand has been driving since he was seventeen. I don't tell Nick or any of my friends about my new young coach. Nick comes home late because he's often travelling up north with a new client, sometimes staying up there. I am a different me with Charlie, and I want to keep it this way.

Weeks later, when I manage to park in a bay without a single mistake, I hug Charlie. He looks so proud of me. The second time I manage it, he reaches out and I kiss him on the cheek. Then, I lean in just a little, and our lips meet and I feel alive. The third time when I conquer my worst fear, reversing around the corner, we go to his flat. Inside, I hesitate for a moment. He whispers, 'I never thought someone like you would be here with me.' He fawns on my body. With no child to pamper, I had pampered myself. I am on top of him, and as I move up and down, he says, 'Just look at the light reflecting off your pendant.' It's my diamond pendant. 'Beautiful, everything about you is beautiful. Lit up.' He traces shapes on my skin, exclaiming at the honey brownness.

A successful parallel park results in doing it against the wall. He lifts my skirt over my knees, my knickers fall around my black sling-back shoes. 'Don't leave me,' he says, hugging my legs. Sometimes we play music. *Je t'aime, Je t'aime* Serge Gainsbourg sings on a rainy, dreamy evening. Sometimes we cook. We eat bowls of spaghetti, sitting on his bed, drinking wine out of the bottle.

I stop worrying that soon I will be thirty-seven. I stop counting days like a machine. I don't force Nick to have sex on all the fertile days in a cycle, like I used to, so he doesn't have to plan his travel around my ovulation cycle. He is delighted about my improved parking skills.

All Charlie wants is me. Coming in from behind, he kisses me harder.

'Come away with me. We will go away, live in a cottage far away.'

'The young and their dreams,' I say.

He wants me to forget what I should do, what I must do.

'Why don't you dream?'

But how can it be? Our lives are different, worlds apart, tectonic plate shifting, fusing, breaking away. There's Nick, the man I met when I came to London to study, the reason I am in this country. There's all we have built together and all that we plan to do, as parents. Yet if we never become parents, do we have a reason to be together? That question bursts open in my mind and like a weed it grows, just like the guilt. I imagine telling Nick. The anger, the derision. 'A delivery van driver, better than me?!' And Charlie, he thinks the world of me but he's so young. And is he serious?

Suddenly it is October. I realise a month has passed and my period hasn't come. The ovulation predictor kits come with a pregnancy stick and I have several sitting in a drawer. Do I even dare? I take it out. I hide in the bathroom. It shows two lines double pink. I rush to show Nick, a drop of wee still sitting on the white plastic. He laughs like he hasn't in years. The GP confirms the pregnancy. Thirty-four weeks to go.

I calculate the dates in my head, trying to go back to that moment I conceived. And with whom. I worry. Charlie and I were careful so it couldn't be, it just couldn't. I had read somewhere that you get pregnant when your subconscious really wants to. In one of those moments with Charlie, his perfectly formed smooth body, his hands, his lips, his legs around mine, had I allowed myself to get pregnant? The sex with Nick was perfectly planned however, the right date, the right time. Were babies conceived in passion or in planning?

I must tell Charlie. I want to talk it out, to see what he thinks. We are meeting the following day. But he doesn't come. There's no message from him until late that night.

Uma, got to talk.

Sure, when?

There's no response after that.

He calls the next day. 'I am sorry. I want to meet you but you know…my girlfriend, she's suddenly come back. She's missed me. We need to talk. I do want to see you, Ooma, I am just trying to figure things out. I miss you. But I've known her since I was twenty and I …'

'Hey, it's good. Don't worry. Call me later,' I say.

I imagine his dimples flash, his face relax. 'We will catch up soon, OK?'

I don't tell him my news.

A month later, I see him at the retail park. There's a girl with him, young, tattooed, dark-haired. He sees me, comes over. He has a place on the course he wanted. Design technology. He owes me. How will he ever thank me?

I smile. I see the smile in his eyes. Maybe he notices my very slight bump?

They have the same colouring, Charlie and Nick. Dark brown hair. Dark eyes. But I will know. The moment my baby is born I will know from the eyes. I caress my stomach. Surely I will know.

MATAR PANEER FOR THE LIVING

Radhika Kapur

When Nidhi Chachi has guests over, the maid quietly slides into the gleaming living room, a cool marble temple where the searing summer heat dares not enter, balancing water glasses atop a tray in her fuchsia-bangled hands. Heaven forbid that the water level in the glasses isn't equal; if it isn't, she is sent back to the kitchen to correct her mistake. Nidhi Chachi can also discuss the cut of okra – straight versus diagonal – for hours, like it's normal dinner table conversation. Her hawk-eyes can spot the slightest speck of rebellious dust under the curved foot of the rosewood dining table and she hollers for the maid to come with a delicate paintbrush to clean it. At once.

*

As was the custom, after the funeral we had congregated at Mataji's home where she had lived with her only daughter, my distantly-related aunt, Anju Bua. A grand old stalwart of the family, Mataji had succumbed to old age and was cremated at the electric crematorium on Lodhi Road where everyone in the family is cremated. It's in a nice part of Delhi where death hobnobs with designer stores selling sheer chiffons and backless blouses. Here, grief is well turned out. Not everyone wears white, like in Bollywood movies, but dull crispness is considered quite appropriate. I, however, was in white, thanks to my mother.

'These jeans are ok for your theatre-veatre group, but not for a funeral, Savi. Here, wear this,' she said, whipping out a white salwar kameez from the stack in her cupboard. She buys white salwar-kameezes whenever she thinks a relative is about to die – sometimes years before they actually do. She gets terribly excited when someone pops it.

'Weddings and funerals. When else does the entire family get together,' she would sigh.

No food could be cooked in the house where a death had occurred for four days. It was up to the relatives to file in with casseroles filled with piping hot curries. I knew the drill. I had heaved the fifty paranthas and tangy potatoes my mother had made with frenzied zeal into the car. Nidhi Chachi brought the matar paneer curry.

Nidhi Chachi whispered to me that someone had stolen the paneer from the matar paneer. 'Someone' of course was code for 'maid'. My aunt has a love-hate relationship with maids. She loves to hate them. I managed to not laugh – it would have been inappropriate at such a time.

Anju Bua sobbed softly, leaning against the calming caress of a velvet sofa. Her sobs were sucked into the cuboid desert cooler and dripped down the khus mats on its sides. An impressively large picture of Mataji's smiling face looked benevolently, down upon us out of an ornate photo frame. Riotous orange marigolds, that grace both weddings and funerals, garlanded it. The tip of an incense stick glowed red and a brass oil lamp flickered. The place smelt like a temple – ghee, jasmine and gentle khus snaking through the air. When she was alive, Mataji had smelt of turmeric, cumin and Keo Karpin hair oil.

Relatives huddled on a white sheet protecting a silk carpet, hugging their creaky knees to their chest. Chacha, bored out of his bald head, played Candy Crush with his fingers sliding obsessively over his phone. Others chatted quietly, sharing anecdotes about Mataji and when they ran out of those, 'What else is happening these days?' My mother shone with sorrow. It lit her up from within like a slithery brass lamp. Her fingertips thrummed with solicitousness and she squeezed Anju Bua's shoulder just a bit too hard. Anju Bua moved away deftly and gazed at a marble-top side table where her father's photo rested. A porcelain figurine, a Japanese woman in a Kimono, kept him frozen company. A cry escaped Anju Bua's chest, before she pressed a fist to her lips.

'You know I can't remember the smell of Daddy's aftershave anymore. Soon, I will forget Ma's hair oil too. I could smell it every time I pinned on her artificial juda. Always wanted to look tip-top, Ma, even if she had nowhere to go. That's the most terrible thing. Not the person dying, but the memory dying. Then what is left?'

'You will not forget it, Anju,' my mother said. 'Be strong'. It was mandatory to dole out philosophical advice on such occasions. Don't cry, trust in God, Krishna says the body is discarded like clothes, but the soul never dies, no one goes before their time. It doesn't matter what the advice is, whether it actually helps, whom it helps but it's something to say at a time when no one knows what to say.

A wave of dread washed over my throat and my stomach clenched. What would I forget? The softness of my mother's hand when she stroked my hair? The shape of the mole on my father's neck? Was I the only one who felt fear? Had all the other older relatives attended so many of these events, that death had become that ugly vase in the cabinet that no one notices anymore? Nidhi Chachi stalked past me and interrupted my contemplation. Her swinging dupatta, like the wave of a hand, hailed our urgent attention, as she marched towards Anju Bua. She descended onto her expensive haunches and clasped her hands tight. Her breath unfurled.

'Anju, the maid has stolen the paneer from the matar paneer.' Her eyes were hard like the diamond flowers blooming in her earlobes. They met lost, unfocussed ones. Pools of sadness.

'Ma never liked paneer.'

'We must do something about it.'

'You know, Ma said she must be a fake Punjabi. For not liking paneer! I mean which Punjabi doesn't, right?' Anju bua spat out a forced, jovial laugh.

'How can she do such a thing on this day of all days,' demanded Nidhi Chachi.

Anju Bua's eyes welled up.

'It's fine. How can I eat paneer when Ma didn't?' She turned her face away from Nidhi Chachi.

'It's not fine.' Chachi's voice crashed into the walls. A gasp. Perhaps it was mine. Every eye in the room was fixed on Nidhi

Chachi's curling lips. Even the Japanese figurine's glass eyes. Chacha was no longer playing Candy Crush. He had just found something else on which to fasten his glazed look.

Nidhi Chachi swallowed as she realised it wasn't acceptable to shout at a grieving woman.

'All I am saying is that we must not let her get away with it. You leave it to me. It's too much for you.' Her voice rustled, soft and synthetic like a nylon sari. You know the ones given to cleaners and cooks on Diwali. Cheap and shiny fire hazards.

A fair plump foot with painted pink nails stepped across the threshold, breaking the knife-edge tension. Mrs Mehra, the neighbour, it seems, rolled into the room, followed by her husband, wailing through her rosy lips.

'*Behenji chali gayi*! She's gone!'

Anju Bua's sobs escaped. Her grief was wild and uninhibited like the Ganga. I noticed wet eyes and dabbed dupattas. Mum quickly asked me to get water. Water to calm water.

Nidhi Chachi pivoted. Relatives tilted their knees and toes out of her unstoppable path. She drew closer and closer to the kitchen. I followed behind, curiously, empty glass in hand.

The matar paneer was bubbling on the hob along with the other food. Nidhi Chachi fixed her police inspector-stare on Barfi, the cook.

'The paneer seems less.' She looked at the wok with nonchalance, eyebrows raised in curiosity as fake as the designer sunglasses sold on the pavement in Connaught Place. *Gucci-Prada 200-300, Gucci Prada 200-300.* Barfi's lips tightened. Her hand stirring the matar paneer paused. She shrugged, 'I don't know, this is how it came. I'm just heating it for lunch.'

'No, no, there were more paneer pieces in it, I'm sure,' insisted Nidhi Chachi.

'Ask the guests. Maybe someone was hungry and ate some?'

'Did you eat any?' There it was, out in the open, the accusation that had lurked behind those Bobbi Brown lips.

Barfi's head jerked.

'Hain? Why would I eat it? All I have eaten since this morning is an omelette and the leftover bread, *bas.*'

'But someone has.'

Barfi yanked a bottle of turmeric from a shelf and slammed it on the kitchen surface. Clouds of deep yellow exploded inside it. She removed jars of cumin, red chilies, coriander powder and fennel. She dragged a duster back and forth over the grainy spice shelf. Her arms became a blur, multiple arms, Durga arms.

'Can I control who comes in here? Maybe someone came and ate some. I don't know. It looks like the same amount of paneer to me. I have worked in this house for so many years. If I had to steal something, why would I steal panee*r?* I would steal something more valuable!'

Nidhi Chachi's eyebrows collided with her hairline.

'Really?'

'Madam's gold chain lies in the bathroom on many days. She forgets it after her bath. I give it to her.' Barfi thumped her chest.

I don't think Nidhi Chachi liked that. She yanked open the fridge door bearing an OM magnet under which fluttered a home delivery menu for Gupta's Vegetarian Paradise. She scanned the refrigerator's shiny white insides, shifting aside utensils, her large bum sticking out. She emerged from its cool, bulb-lit interiors.

'So that the day you take it, she doesn't suspect you huh?

Clever. Where have you hidden the paneer? In some plastic bag? In a tiffin? Let's check.'

'Chachi!', the word dislodged from my throat like a bone from a choking man's mouth. 'This isn't American immigration!'

Barfi turned to stare Chachi in the eye. Her big round bindi flashed fire from the centre of her eyebrows. She switched off the gas. Till then, I didn't know switching off the gas could be a war cry. I felt like reciting the Durga Saptashati. *Rupam Devi, Barfi Devi, Yasho Devi, Barfi Devi.*

'That's it! I will not listen to this.' She stalked out, crushing the innocent baby cockroach crawling its way across the tiled floor under her merciless rubber Hawai chappal.

'Hey where are you going?' Nidhi Chachi cried.

'To find another job. The poor don't have much, but we do have our dignity.' She disappeared into the bleached sun-lit world beyond the door.

Nidhi Chachi stood in front of my red-eyed Bua, looking everywhere but at her. She gazed nervously at the Kimono lady, at the antique silver fan framed grandly on the wall and finally at the book, 'Consciousness and the Soul' that the Mehras had given to my aunt and which was lying listlessly on her lap. I couldn't wait to see what would happen next. Nidhi Chachi cleared her throat.

'Er…she's gone,' she said.

'Huh?' queried Anju Bua.

'The maid, she's gone. Quit, I think. Call her tomorrow, when she cools off. I am sure she will come back. She has a nasty temper.'

'What do you mean she's gone?'

Anju Bua's breath curdled. Her white dupatta spilled out of her clenched fist, a wrinkled mess. She snatched short, shallow breaths. She was a full-blown neon-lit mata ki chowki. This is when calm, dutiful housewives turn into fiery viragos, tossing their hair wildly as the Goddess descends into their bodies. I used to imitate them as a child. *Mata chad gayi.*

Everyone snapped into action.

'Be strong, Anju,' Nidhi Chachi said sternly. 'Try to stay in control.'

My mother pushed the glass of water into Bua's hands.

'Drink drink.' The glass shook, water sloshed, her teeth chattered like a watchman's on a Neel Kamal plastic chair on a cold winter night, ashes of a long-doused fire at his feet. Bored Chacha got off Candy Crush.

'She needs a doctor. I'll go get one!'

'Her food, her food,' cried Anju Bua, rocking back and forth. Her words circular and repetitive like prayer beads.

'Who Barfi's,' asked my mother.

'No ma's.'

'What about it?'

'I can't lose it.'

'Why will you?'

'Barfi is the one who knows the recipes!'

'I am sure you do too,' my mother said in the same reassuring voice as when I was ten and hysterically convinced that a watermelon was going to grow inside me because I had swallowed its seed. It didn't work then, it didn't work now.

'I can't lose her food, her taste, her flavours. She lives in them.' Anju Bua wept like I had expected her to weep at the crematorium.

We tried calling Barfi, but she didn't answer. We meaning, me. Anything to do with technology was relegated to the youngest person in the room. Her ringtone, a bawdy Bollywood song, made me think about her sex life and whether it was any good. Nidhi Chachi said she would apologise, even though it was Barfi who had an attitude problem. Anju Bua gripped the grey Pashmina someone draped around her. It was hard to say where her face ended and the shawl began. They were both the same colour.

Mataji had been a legendary cook. Her biryanis, shammi kebabs and lehsun-vale aloo were the stuff to break allegiances. Voting day dinner at her home was a family tradition. But only those who voted for the Congress were invited. She would preside over her table in an elegant sari and matching beads. Last year, even Bored Chacha who always votes BJP, couldn't stay away. Of course he lied and swore he voted for her handsome heartthrob, Rahul Gandhi, the heir to the Congress party.

Suddenly, Anju Bua pushed herself up like she had seen a film star. She rushed into her mother's now empty room, a cavalcade of relatives behind her. She grabbed the hair oil bottle from the dresser. The comb next to it still had strands of Mataji's hair in it. She sank onto her mother's bed, hugging the bottle close. 'When did I have the time? Ma taught Barfi all her recipes.' She glanced at the bottle as if her mother resided in it – in that tiny green Keo Karpin hair oil container. The cloying smell was familiar. It had sunk into Mataji's soft, loose skin, her pillow, her clothes, her hugs.

Anju Bua's husband had died young.

'Heart Attack. Here one minute, gone the next. They should

60

have gone to hospital sooner, but he wanted to finish watching Santa Barbara. We had just started getting foreign shows in those days,' my mother would recount in her colourful telling of the tale. Having to provide for herself for the first time, Anju Bua became a busy real estate agent.

Now that I think of it, I had never seen her in the kitchen, only on the phone to her clients. I didn't know my mother's recipes, especially her Sunday mutton curry, I thought to myself. Learn it, Babe, learn it. It was the taste of home. I would be homeless without it.

The doctor arrived, a briefcased one, the kind who took your pulse and looked like he gave out medicines in pudiyas, a dying breed of family physicians. He prescribed a sleeping pill. Mum tucked Anju Bua into bed like a child, clucking and fussing.

Nidhi Chachi went back to doing what she did best. She ran her finger over the door frame and showed her dusty finger to Bored Chacha.

'See she doesn't even dust properly. I say it's good she went.'

My mother joined the Mehras. 'Savi,' she yelled across the room, beckoning me over. She proceeded to ask them if they knew of any potential grooms for me, despite me hissing, 'Mum, this is not the place.' Mrs Mehra offered to pass on a boy her own daughter had rejected. 'Because he didn't know where Big Chill restaurant was! Can you believe it? I don't know how these children will ever get married.' She shook her head sadly, tut-tutting, then slid her evangelist eyes my way, 'But show her his photo. After all, no good boy should go to waste.' My mother nodded emphatically and rallied, 'Yes, Mrs Mehra! No good boy should go to waste.' It sounded like a prize-winning slogan, one of those where you win a Sumeet mixie or washing machine.

The next morning, we came bearing tender aubergine bharta and pulao rice. At 10.32 am, the doorbell rang. It was Barfi. Hearing her voice, Anju Bua leap-frogged over spiritual books and cross-legged mourners. She leapt towards her and clasped her to her chest like a lost lover.

'I thought you had gone,' she wailed.

'Where would I go? This is my home! I don't remember any other.'

They clung to each other like a shirt to a sweaty body in the oppressive July heat and wept. Outside, the koyal cooed. Shockingly happy laburnum flowers rained yellow.

LUCKY GIRL

Catherine Menon

On bad days, Shosha knows her children, with all their shining flaws, have always been inevitable. Jimmy, for example, had his roots in the Christmas lucky dip at her convent school in rural Malaysia nearly twenty-five years ago. She was the only Indian girl in the class and she'd never won anything before, but this time she took the prize: a nativity peg-doll set that had turned out – *a factory-mistake only*, the businessman donor said defensively, *nothing to be done about it* – to be completely blank. No painted faces on those dolls, no blue shawl for Mary, and little Jesus as empty-faced as a blown egg. What a *lucky* girl, though, the teacher had cooed, but Shosha had stared with disappointment. She'd tried to draw the features onto the dolls later, from her paint-box. It hadn't been a success.

That's how she thinks of the children on bad days: factory-mistakes. Five-year-old Jimmy certainly has features, he has large eyes and fair, beautiful skin like the small boys she fell in love with as a narrow-eyed, dark-skinned small girl. But Jimmy is beyond all instruction, or all that she can give him, which is much the same thing. Jimmy *refuses*. He has the blankness of

63

that long-ago Joseph peg-doll and its resistance to all her improvements. From the moment Jimmy was born, he's been his own person. Shosha might be *his* mother, Jimmy allows when labelling the people in his crayoned pictures, but he crumples in rage at the suggestion he's her son.

Prinny's quieter than Jimmy, she's more pliable and she's more clearly Shosha's fault. But Prinny's flaws, too, began before she was born. When Shosha was seven years old she'd invented an imaginary friend named Puteri. Once Shosha had conjured Puteri into existence, though, she hadn't known what to do with her. Puteri wouldn't play. She'd stubbornly refuse to appear during the day, and then at night she'd creep out from the darkened almirah or swing herself from the stirring bedroom fan. Shosha began to have nightmares and was scolded and given useless night-lights. After a few months, she took to a kind of nocturnal sternness and learnt to turn Puteri back into a fold of mosquito net or her own crumpled uniform. On these bad days, these factory-mistake days, she wishes she could do the same to her daughter. *Prinny.* Shosha regrets calling her that now. Prinny. Princess. It seems to her to be a temporary name, a name for something which might be taken away at any moment. Princesses are ethereal as candyfloss. They could melt in the rain or drift away into strangers' cars or get called upon by social services when a teacher notices the marks of Shosha's fingers on their small thin arms. Princesses can't be trusted.

*

Shosha came over to England from Malaysia with her husband Naresh. He was her second husband; she was his first wife. Naresh

64

used to introduce her that way, when she met his friends. Later, he stopped introducing her altogether. She'll always be his first wife, though. Like her own children, she has the bruises to show for it.

Back then, she hadn't believed bad days could happen in England. She knows better now. The thin, chilled English air seals up all her good intentions like tight-fitted window glass and her bad days here are worse than they ever were in Malaysia. This particular day starts at eight in the morning when she's already late for work. She tugs the yellow curtains back in the flat's tiny bedroom and sees the window panes smeared with dirty rain.

"No! It isn't *time*."

Jimmy burrows his head under the blankets, while Prinny clings to her with starfish arms. Shosha promises sweets if they get up and smacks if they don't. She never makes good on either the promise or the threat, and so the children have learnt to simply ignore her. Finally, she cajoles them into the bathroom. A quick wash, into their shirts, their trousers, their inside-out-and-difficult socks, and all the time she's wishing that she could turn the key and leave them both in the bathroom forever. She supposes they feel the same about her.

And at the back of her mind, dully, she thinks about leaving. She's thought about leaving for nearly as long as she can remember, as far back as the convent school and those large-eyed, fair-skinned boys she kissed in the flame tree behind her grandmother's house. She used to dream about growing up and getting on a train and rushing down all the way to KL. Things would be different there, she knew. And then one day she did grow up and get on a train to KL, and didn't stop rushing until she arrived in London, where everything was very different indeed. She could cry, sometimes, at how different everything had become.

Her grandparents gave in once, taking her to KL as a treat. All she remembers about it is a poster pinned up outside an MRT station advertising a circus. *Elephants and bears*, it read, *Strongmen! Shocks!* She'd been entranced.

These days, though, she's used to shocks and she's had more than enough of men – strong or not – to last her a few years. But she still dreams of running away; she dreams of joining the circus and taming bears. But she can't, not really. The children are in the way. Jimmy and Prinny wouldn't suit circus life. They'd ladder her spangled tights, they'd drop the juggle balls, they'd scream just when the bears were about to dance. Her love for them is like a dirty blanket over her head, or a weight about her neck. Running away, she sees, will have to be done differently now. With a railway crossing, she'd thought once, a dark and desperate thought when she found out she was pregnant with Jimmy. With a steep cliff, she'd thought when Prinny began to kick, or the sort of coat with deep enough pockets for riverbed stones.

Once the children are dressed, she sits then down on the stained couch for breakfast. They don't want to eat. They aren't hungry or perhaps, like Shosha herself, they're hoping for something better from today than own-brand Weetabix.

"I don't want breakfast! I want to be in bed. I want to be at nursery with Prinny," Jimmy howls, adding for good measure, "I don't want to be here!"

Nor do I, Shosha feels like telling him, but she still has today sufficiently under control to recognise that as a bad decision. To comfort them, she offers to tell them a story. They love her stories – far more, she thinks, than they've ever loved her. So they splash their spoons in the cereal bowls and spill their milk while she tells them about the flame trees behind her grandmother's house and the convent school. They clamber over the sofa arms while she talks about the train that went all the way to KL, and then they abandon their breakfasts completely when she tells them about the circus. They leap about in their too-small pyjamas with their hands held up like paws, knocking the kitchen chairs over. There are tears and Shosha thinks *serves you right*. She should have kept the bears for herself.

Shosha never tells the children stories about England. They live here, after all, they know better than to be charmed by it. Jimmy, with his odd grown-up wisdom, is already past the reach of charm and as for Prinny, she'll no doubt hear enough stories before she's her mother's age. Stories from boys with night-before eyes, stories from men old enough to be her father. Shosha wishes she could give Prinny some good advice, but perhaps her daughter, like her son, is already long past that.

She usually takes the children to the council nursery straight after breakfast, coming back afterwards to the flat to get ready for work. Today, though, the effort of getting them out of the door exhausts her. Instead, she hands them both a bar of chocolate from the corner shop and lets them thunder back into the bedroom while she slumps at the table again. There's a package of chocolate-chip cookies in the shopping she still hasn't unpacked from last night and she begins to eat her methodical way through them. The pasty dough soothes her; the way each chew and swallow is exactly the same as the last. In Malaysia, she had nasi lemak for breakfast, or kari ayam so spicy it would bring tears to her eyes. In England, she makes do with cookies.

She eats her way through the whole package, watching the

clock incuriously. She ought to be vacuuming the kitchenette floor right now at the office or doing the hourly check of the ladies' toilets. She likes to chat while she works, she likes to tell the receptionists about a new-build flat she's buying or tell the in-house solicitors how she'd been accepted at Oxford to study law herself. The solicitors finish their tea hastily and the receptionists noisily wash their hands and retreat to their bank of telephones. Shosha, left alone, gnaws at her glass bangles. The things she says aren't true, of course, any more than the bears are true – anymore than anything she wants – but they might be, she tells herself defiantly. She is, after all, a lucky girl.

Munching the last cookie, she crumples up the packaging. By now she's so late that it's nearly stopped being a problem and become something else, more like a treat. She walks around the kitchen feeling untethered, and takes a pack of cigarettes from the cupboard. Her grandmother would have been horrified to see her smoking, once she'd got over being horrified by everything else about Shosha. In fact, Shosha doesn't even smoke all that much but she does like the paraphernalia: the tobacco, the little filter tips and paper, and *have you got a light? Can I have one of yours?* She starts conversations this way with people who look interesting. She started the children this way.

The noise from the bedroom has quietened down. Through the open door she can see Jimmy sprawled on his back on the bed with Prinny curled against him. They're nearly asleep again after the early morning and all that sugar. She ought to hurry them together, collect her umbrella and apron, get her apologies ready and her life in order. But she doesn't. She quietly walks to the bedroom door and closes it before slipping the cigarettes into the pocket of her jeans.

She slips her shoes on, then pulls the front door to the flat open, stepping out into the corridor. It's a very English way to live, with everyone and their belongings firmly locked away. The hallways have vinyl floors and cold, frosted windows with the sort of glass she couldn't break, no matter how much she tried. From out here she can hear the rush-hour traffic, all those buses packed full of people on legitimate journeys. Shosha's learnt to like buses: the polite murmur as someone lurches into her, the tiny shifts and slips of the other passengers. She's learnt to like touching at arms-length.

She closes the door to her flat behind her and takes a cigarette from the packet. Smoking always makes her feel romantic. With a cigarette between her lips and a drink in her hand, she's playing at being a different person. One with more, or perhaps less, to offer. One who fits neatly into this English hallway and those English buses. She's so engrossed in this thought that it isn't until she's on the ground floor that she puts her hand in her pocket again and realises she's forgotten her key.

For a moment she doesn't move, her cigarette still in her mouth. More than anything, she wants to keep on walking. She even tries it, a few steps that feel weighty, like they might become *where it all began.* The start of her new life, outside an MRT station or on a bus or in a three-ring circus and here, she frowns. Stops walking. She has the children, of course, her inevitable children. Sighing, she lets the cigarette drop from her lips onto the floor and swivels the toe of her shoe on it. When it's been ground into tiny flakes she turns around and climbs back up the stairs. She's slower this time, and by the time she reaches her flat she can feel sweat beneath her arms.

"Jimmy?" She taps on the door, then hits it more sharply. "Jimmy! Can you open the door?"

There's no answer. The children will be deeply asleep by now, arms and legs splayed out. Shosha sags against the wall, sliding down until her knees press against her chest. She thumps the door again, a flat, open-palmed slap.

"Hello?"

The door of the flat next to hers opens and old Mr Rahman peers out. He must have been listening; he always does. He leaves her reproachful notes about the noise from her flat, or the visitors she has late at night and the way they leave the building door wide open as they stride manfully away. He says these things are a problem but Shosha envies him. She would prefer to be living next door to her life, too.

"Miss Varghese, is everything all right..." He doesn't finish the sentence, letting the words fade away, and she bristles.

"I was just on my way to work," she blurts out, and stares at him defiantly as though that might make it true.

Mr Rahman blinks, looking befuddled and doubtful. In the chilly light he looks dishevelled and old, as though he's just come from a secret nap or a secret vice. He tried, shyly, talking to her in Hindi – or maybe Punjabi or Urdu; how was she to know the difference? – when she'd first moved in. It had been like a private message, one she didn't understand, but she can't blame him. In England, people who look like her come from Karachi or Delhi or even Birmingham. She once spent a whole evening talking to a portly, sweating HR manager about the Mumbai slum where she'd grown up. It had only seemed polite.

Remembering that moment of missed connection now, with Mr Rahman's muddled buttons and skewed collar right in front of her, makes her feel suddenly, unbearably tender. She wants to take his hand; she wants to kiss his forehead and fetch him a pair of slippers and see if together they can't perhaps break those frosted corridor windows after all. *Shall we run away together*, she'd ask him. *Shall we go to Karachi or KL or even perhaps Birmingham? Shall we join the circus? Shall we never come back?*

"I've locked myself out," she explains instead, and he sighs.

"I'll ring a locksmith." After a pause, he adds, "You'd better come in."

He holds the door to his flat open, looking reluctant. She gazes about her with pleasure as she walks through. He keeps it very clean, she notices, although there's a mirrored, grimy look to the furniture as though he's polished over the dirt. The floor's bare, and the air smells tantalisingly of incense and sandalwood soap. It smells like home. A picture on the wall shows a young man in a graduation gown – a grandson? A son – behind glass that's filmy from being wiped over and over again. She regards the picture curiously. The young man doesn't look much like Mr Rahman, not up close. Something about him, in fact, reminds Shosha of KL, of convent school, of fair-skinned large-eyed boys in the flame trees.

"Telephone, telephone…" Mr Rahman is puffing, bent double and rummaging in a cupboard for a telephone directory.

"Quickly, please," he tells the locksmith, "the young lady's dropped her children at nursery and she was on her way back out to work".

She doesn't contradict him. She rather likes this better Shosha he's speaking of, this Shosha for whom today is firmly under control.

"Would you like a cup of tea?" he asks, rather reluctantly.

"Yes, please," she says, hoping to see his kitchen. She's curious about other people's possessions, likes seeing how they slice their

71

sandwiches or brush their hair. She picks up their habits when she can, the way she sometimes copies how people talk. She gets along better, somehow, when she isn't being herself.

Mr Rahman walks stiffly out of the room. She hears a milk steamer, hears the crisp, clean clink of metal on glass. When he comes back, he's holding two milky, frothed cups of tea and the air about him is cushioned and warmed with spices.

"Try this," he tells her. "It's called teh tarik. It's a drink from Malaysia. My wife used to…she was Malaysian."

She reaches out and takes one of the cups. She thinks she might cry. Teh tarik and the hot, fresh smell of roti canai from hawker stalls. The muddy river at the back of her grandmother's house, the canna lilies that were so red they hurt her eyes. A different Shosha, before buses and cleaning shifts. Before the children, before the children even seemed inevitable.

Mr Rahman pinches the neat crease on the knees of his trousers and lowers himself into the armchair. He's wearing a hearing aid, she sees. It nestles baby-pink behind his ear, looking startlingly new against his shaved-yesterday face.

"The locksmith shouldn't be long," he says, encouragingly, after a few seconds' silence. "I hope you don't have far to go for work?"

"Oh, no," she replies. "I work in the City. A law firm."

His eyes are large and blinking with a kind of snuffling trust. "A lawyer, hanh? Your parents must be very proud."

Those large eyes of his slide over to the picture of the young man on the wall. A flawless son, the kind of child to shine brightly under glass. Shosha swallows.

"Yes, I was accepted to Oxford." The words come easily and naturally.

He nods, his head tilted with the hearing aid towards her, as though he doesn't want to miss a single word. He doesn't raise his eyebrows like the receptionists at work do when she says these things, or frown reprovingly like the solicitors. He believes her, simply and wholeheartedly; the same kind of belief she used to have in her imaginary friends and her peg-dolls. A blunt kind of misery rises up inside her. Like a princess, she oughtn't to be trusted.

"And I'm thinking of buying a new-build flat," she blurts out.

Her voice is louder than before, and Mr Rahman looks up with a startled expression. But now that she's begun, she can't quite stop. Her law degree, her new-build flat, her children who are in the top stream at school and have never, ever been slapped. Mr Rahman listens, his wrinkled hands wrapped tight around his glass, nodding at every word. He asks questions – kind, weak questions, the sort she didn't think men asked – and she watches the lamp cup palmfuls of light onto his wispy hair.

"How wonderful to have these clever children," he says. "They must take after you."

She flinches. That isn't a compliment, not to a woman like Shosha. It's a prediction, it's a wicked-witch curse. It's uncalled-for and she bristles. *They must take after you.*

"My own Mohammad, my son," Mr Rahman says confidingly, "he –"

There's a thump from next door, from her own flat. It rattles the walls, shaking Mohammad behind his glass.

"What's that?" Mr Rahman's voice is sharp. "Is that from your flat?"

Shosha shakes her head, and they hear another thud. A trail of footsteps next door, galloping their way from Shosha's bedroom to her kitchen.

"Your children, Miss Varghese…they're not in there, are they? By themselves?"

The children. Poor gifted, slapped children who must take after her, who must, whatever else they might have wanted. Mr Rahman has set her children's little feet on Shosha's own path, as though the words mean nothing at all. She no longer wants to cry; she wants revenge.

"No," she says firmly. "The children aren't at home."

"But…"

There's another series of thumps next door and then a voice raised in a howl of rage. There's a clanging of metal on tiles. Prinny must have got into the kitchen cupboards, and she's banging the pots together. Clever little bear, thinks Shosha.

"Mum!" It's Jimmy's voice, filtering through the wall.

"Miss Varghese…" Mr Rahman's lips mash together, "that *is* them. Next door."

She folds her arms, gives him a vicious smile and shakes her head slightly. Mr Rahman will have no part in her children, not even the knowledge of them, not if Shosha can help it. He should never have believed her in the first place.

When the telephone rings they both jump. Mr Rahman quickly picks up the receiver, giving her a polite, nervous nod.

"Yes? Hello?" He covers the phone. "It's the locksmith. He's here."

Now that she has to go, she doesn't want to. She wants, perversely, to stay with Mr Rahman in this clean, empty flat and clean, empty life. They could slip out in their socked feet together and leave her children and his dead wife to sort out the mess. They could be lawyers together, they could be strong men, they could be stones in a coat pocket or a bottle of the kind of sleeping pills you shouldn't mix with alcohol. They could be bears.

"You should go, Miss Varghese." He's holding the door open for her, ushering her out. In the corridor, a young man is already working on her lock. He has an unlit cigarette in his mouth and he's fattish, with a puffy back that bulges from his t-shirt and over his belt of tools. He grunts as she comes out. "One sec, love."

He levers a tiny metal screwdriver upwards and her door clicks open. Jimmy rushes out into the corridor. He must have been pressing against the doorframe with all his strength.

"Mummy!"

Prinny follows him. They're both in tears, barging against her as though they want to be back underneath her skin. Like peg-dolls, she thinks, like invisible friends. It's far too late to wish them away now.

"You should have said there were kids inside," the locksmith says accusingly.

He stands up, those competent fingers slotting everything back into his tool belt. He looks like an adult, in the same way that Naresh did, in the way that Shosha herself somehow doesn't and never has.

"That's twenty pounds." He looks at her severely.

The children stay silent, creeping behind her like footprints as she goes inside for her purse. When she puts the money into his hand he shakes himself like a dog after a cold bath. "Be more careful," he mutters at her, without meeting her eyes.

When he's gone, she hugs the children, suddenly and fiercely. She takes them back inside the flat and gathers them up into her arms as though she'll never let them go. At lunchtime, she picnics with them out of the shopping bags she still hasn't put away. They ask her for stories but she shakes her head, letting them bang pots on the floor instead and run races across the living room. Nobody eats Weetabix or bathes or goes to work, and they romp until after midnight when Jimmy suddenly snarls at her, "Why don't you *ever* put us to bed?"

She'd still like to run away, she knows. She still wants to be a different Shosha, to be a first wife again living in a new-build flat paid for with her Oxford law degree. She still wants an escape from her factory-errors and her frosted-glass life, but she knows better by now. She isn't the kind to escape after all. She's the kind who stays put, the kind who makes do with her own lucky mistakes, with her neighbours and locksmiths and children and bears.

LOST FOR WORDS

Deblina Chakrabarty

' . . . I stop talking now.
I work, then I read,
cotching under a lantern hooked to the mast.

I try to forget what happiness was,
and when that don't work, I study the stars.'

It surprised him to have these shards of Derek Walcott's poetry surface to the rim of his lips. He hadn't found the words to speak for a very long time. Her patchwork skirt must've been the trigger. A symbol of careless gaiety from another time when colours could be thrown together and someone could stitch a whimsical garment out of it. It wasn't just the skirt though, it was her. Everything about her seemed displaced. Not from here or now.

He recalled the first time he had noticed her. It was on his nicotine break at work in the slick glass vestibule that snaked around his squat office building. Smoking was one of those habits that had carried over, albeit in an updated electronic avatar. She stood at a distance, half-turned away from him. Her upturned nose and slightly open mouth in sharp profile against the chrome and glass on the landscape, one of those old-fashioned tobacco cigarettes affixed to her lips. She looked alive and whole against the inanimate silvery-grey pallor of the row of identical cuboid buildings, smoke billowing out of her nostrils. He realised it was the first time in ages he had noticed or seen someone's mouth. Masks had been common for so long that people had stopped looking like shuttered shops to him, the way it did in the beginning when it was new.

When the disease started.

Or was it when #wordsareworthmore started?

He didn't remember anymore which came first.

Nobody remembers anymore.

The mouth was deemed a dangerous organ for so long now. It could sneeze, cough, talk, spread rumours, incite riots, start fires, bring down governments, prop up governments, haze students to suicide.

The disease was the first step. Eventually masks went from emergency wear to mandated prohibition to free choice. Surgical and military greys and blacks gave way to pop colours, pithy one-liners, monograms, even Munch's *Scream* for the ones who liked a bit of irony. Once people stopped talking, it only made sense to cover that obsolete organ with decoration, like graffiti on the walls of a deserted, rusty factory.

By the time #wordsareworthmore exploded on street corners, people had already given governments carte blanche to curtail spoken and written words. People were handed out caches of words per month to be portioned between essential communication, work, and a small quota for indulgences; maybe a virtual diatribe one month, maybe poetry or karaoke the next? People realised how efficiently things could run with less talking, writing, reading, and soon words became the indulgence of the leftover people from the other times.

This girl's parted lips in this landscape was like an ice-water bath from the past. Pamela's open lips when he had kissed her on the beach floated into memory, the sun gently setting into the cradle of the horizon. St. Lucia, their honeymoon. He had spent the previous hour reading Walcott in the hammock while Pamela swam. It had been a different silence then. A golden, companionable one, the yin to the yang of speech that would follow as they had a cocktail on the verandah, whispered and made love, dressed to go to dinner. The evening, their lives stretched out before them like the shimmery white sand on the endless beach . . .

*

"Are you new here?' 'he typed into his handset. The words shone up on the flexi-screen affixed to his shirt pocket.

'Three months. I work at UIX in Bot-land. What about you?'

He was taken aback. Did she just spend words on him? A complete stranger? His incredulous look must've given it away.

'Don't worry I have plenty of reserve, I also got a packet as a joining bonus at Bot-land. I need to use them on the bots as well, part of the training and design process. The retro-human models are our bestsellers which means they need to be trained for a relatively large vocabulary and conversation strands.' Her voice was what used to be called chirpy, a laughter hidden around the corner of every 3rd syllable.

'Hi, I'm RM10. I create prototypes and responses at Integrated Interactive Learning – Modern Bionics.'

The words felt halting and alien out of his mouth, he hadn't spoken in such a long while. There hadn't been any need. But her showering him with words at their first interactions made him want to try.

'Ooh that's like top-notch elite stuff! You must be smart,' she continued with a smile. 'The encoded names sound so silly when we speak them aloud, don't they? What were you named?'

Another first in ages. Saying his name aloud. 'Rana,' he smiled.

*

In his memory, his name was conjoined with his mother's kind-eyed smile, crinkly around the edges. He remembered that his name had been her choice, as had been much in his parent's marriage. She had broken with tradition to insist on a two-syllable name for him, easier to pronounce, she had pronounced. The same implacable logic had prevailed when she decided to call Pamela, Pramila. Easier to pronounce she had said, despite the extra letter and the conjunctive syllable. Pamela had nodded and shrugged good-naturedly.

Very little had bothered Pamela; that's what he loved about her. She was like the island breeze; carefree, headed nowhere in particular, tinged with sunshine. Not after their son Ralph died though. She deflated like a hot air balloon soft-landing in a meadow while he caulked like limestone. They bypassed the words and shortcut into a silence they didn't know how to break. Ralph, a loose amelioration of both their names. A single syllable name even approved by his mother. He smiled to himself.

*

'Hi, I'm Rubi,' her smile pulled him from his reverie of the past.

When was the last time a girl's memory followed him home, after Pamela? He couldn't remember. But here was Rubi with her unmasked mouth, her unrationed words, her open smile. He thought he had a generous stash of words stockpiled away – in case of emergency. But 10,000 words a month per person meant you didn't waste them on pleasantries anymore. Doctor's appointments maybe or legal statements, or maybe safe words during BDSM when your other limbs were too restricted to communicate. It was pointless to run over quota and have penalties seep into your Personal Index and be chaperoned by a Bon-itor all month (somebody in the Internal Security department had clearly thought that combining the words 'bot' and 'monitor' was extremely clever!)

Maybe Rubi was interested in him?

Maybe she was just young and unmindful with a free bounty of words to spend.

Something about her caused a flicker, like a candle flame in a darkened room, as he went about his evening routine in automation. The steak grilled to medium-rare accuracy in 3 minutes 12 seconds, the beans blanched in the pan, the potatoes steamed in the cooker. He didn't know what it was, maybe it was her, but today felt like a sauce kind of day.

In the kitchen, what he was unable to do with words, he made up for with his hands. He found the eggs, lemons, vinegar and salt in silent harmony. The soft crack of the shells released the yolks into the bowl and the hand-frother whipped the ingredients into a golden frenzy. Somewhere in the far recesses of the kitchen cabinet he unearthed a long-forgotten jar of poblano peppers, still preserved thanks to the glug of oil in which they floated.

81

They got blitzed in the blender and joined the fresh mayo creating a rich ochre emulsion.

'What culinary bastard have you birthed today?' Pamela would have laughingly asked. She was always amazed at his ability to mix unlikely ingredients into likeable concoctions. Now these kitchen conjurings had become a proxy for expressing dormant feelings; a shorthand to a lost past.

As he settled into his dinner and spooned the rich sauce over his spare, rare steak, tastes, smells and desires came seeping back into his consciousness. That's how little it took; freshly blitzed mayo with preserved peppers . . . . .

*

In the world he was born into, 'ordinary' was a pejorative term, bordering on mild abuse. Ordinary was the specter of an interminable stretch of nothing.

Except that ordinary is temporary. And when it leaves, it doesn't announce its departure with grand cymbals and cacophony, it just slides off, like sheets from naked, sleeping bodies.

When he tried to remember the old, ordinary days with Pamela and Ralph, as a family, his memories flattened into pancakes, the past and further past blended to create static cameos. Pamela, loose-limbed, smiling, her love for black in contrast with her cheery persona. Ralph, with his mop of hair falling sideways in a neat triangle. His own post-doctorate, her startup, Ralph's nursery, pudgy sandcastles flanked by bright orange shovels and buckets during their summer breaks. They had become silent tableaus in the diorama of his past. Had it only been 15 years?

As he was drawn to Rubi and waited to spend a few minutes listening to her chatter or walking her to the air-train, these past memory tableaux started to change. New textures, dimensions and edges spread into his dreams.

There he was, holding Ralph's soft, warm hands at the airport before he boarded the flight to Calcutta to go to his mother who had broken her hip and contracted a chest infection all at the same time.

'Daddy, will you please make jamba rice for me when you come back?'

He had smiled despite himself. There was something to be said for genetic material popping up in the oddest of places. His instinctive cooking had taken the Caribbean jambalaya of their honeymoon and tossed it with smoked sausages, okra, eggs and soya sauce to create a Sino-Portuguese-Caribbean mashup that Pamela had laughed at while scarfing it down. And jamba rice had become a family staple, cooked for comfort, celebration, reassurance and everything in between. But at the airport, bidding reassuring, temporary adieus, they hadn't known that there would be no more jamba rice for their family.

Even then, the lurgy was creeping round the world and shutting down countries, like extinguished streetlights. He stayed suspended with his ill mother halfway across the world, separated from Pamela who sent assurances that she and Ralph were fine. But as borders sealed like par avion envelopes, Ralph fell sick. Just a slight fever, Pamela said cheerfully even as everything around them wobbled like secondhand furniture. In a surreal parallel, his mother slid gently down the slope of consciousness, her breath heaving, her papery palms trembling leaf-like in his hands.

*

'So, who are you then? Like really?', Rubi cast him a mischievous sidelong glance, her face half hidden in the crook of her right arm, her curls falling over it. She was diminutive, lying next to him in their Swiss chalet. It was she who had casually suggested that they visit the Couple o' Hours near their office. All the rooms were individually themed, and Rubi had chosen a Swiss chalet panelled in wood with richly coloured rugs on the leather couch and a knitted comforter on the bed. There was a floor-to-ceiling bookcase and a breathtaking view of the Alps from the deck. As far as simulated nature scenes went, this was one of the better ones. The crackling of the firewood combined with the crisp air from the deck was almost like the real thing, except right here available for a few hours after work rather than having to take flights to foreign countries. Travel had become an antiquity for eccentrics, much like vinyl had been to music when he was young.

'I'm Rana. Like really,' he smiled. He had not spoken for so long that a conversation was a novelty and an exhausting one. But years of silence had made him efficient with minimal words for maximal effect.

'Ok then, what makes you happy, what makes you sad, what are you thinking now?'

'Cooking makes me happy,' he said. You make me happy, he thought. 'Regrets make me sad,' he said. I regret it all, Ralph, Pamela, this silence, this perfect emptiness, he thought. 'And I'm thinking right now that you're very energetic'.' Be careful now, Rana, he thought.

*

There had been no words to tell his dying mother that her grandson had died, his little lungs heaving until they couldn't, much like hers. So he didn't. He remained straitjacketed in the country of his birth while Pamela was alone at their son's funeral. The disease had etched paranoid rules onto human misery. Their calls after that were mostly long ticking silences punctuated by sparse words pulled out with forceps, painfully empty and inadequate. Three weeks later, his mother had died, her rheumy grey eyes glazed over, a gentle smile under the pain on her thin lips. He wrapped up the rituals, her home, his past, in silence while the noise expanded around him and the disease destroyed entire societies. Fearful people were decimated by uncertainty and persuaded by false rhetoric. The streets erupted in protests, marches, tears, commiserations, eulogies around him, and around the world.

No one noticed that he barely said a word.

*

By the time he was able to return home to Pamela, it was winter, outside and within. People on the streets, bound in their coats, scarves and masks, sidestepped more than they walked. Eyes darted in a sea of greyscale and mouths were bound in a pop of false orange gaiety. Ralph's room was as silent as he was. Pamela's black clothes finally synced with her somber silence. They pottered politely around each other for a few months. He didn't know how to reach out to her or let her in. When she told him about those last swift blurry days, they sounded like scenes from a silent horror film. Eventually she went home to her mother in California. She needed the sun, some time, she said. He didn't demur. He had no right, no words, no fight left in him. As the months went by, her trip turned into a break, then a separation and then a parting. He let her go in absentia. Like the rest of his life, quietly and without a fuss.

*

'Would you like to come to my place tonight? It's not as nice as the chalet but it doesn't have a premium if you overstay either!' Rana managed a joke in his text to Rubi to hide his nervousness.

'I'd like that. I've never been to anyone's personal place in this city.' 'Her words glowed in the dark on his screen.

He felt the pace change, a quickening of his heartbeat, a shortening of his breath, the anticipation. It was like an old friend's face, ravaged by time and yet instantly familiar. The sex between him and Rubi had been good, frenetic, endearing even, as she sat face to face with him on her haunches, holding his face, their gaze still and intent in contrast to their undulating bodies. But then the sex was usually good with other women. People fucked to stay sane, some occasionally fucked elaborately when they found the time or the occasion, but sex had long stopped being the marker of relationships, neither a beginning, nor middle nor an end.

But no one had ever come back home. No one had made

him feel alive in the way he was now, smiling, insouciant, bubbling with words.

*

After a long time, today was a jamba rice kind of day. The smell of frying smoked sausages filled the air.

'What's all this?' she asked with a laugh. Her red linen dress clung to her tiny frame.

At his lumbering six feet he towered over her. 'You asked me what makes me happy. This dish makes me happy. I wanted you to share it,' he smiled.

Afterwards as he and Rubi lay spent in his bed, one of Walcott's poems bubbled to his lips. Could he say it out loud?

This coral's shape echoes the hand
It hollowed. Its

Immediate absence is heavy. As pumice,
As your breast in my cupped palm.

Sea-cold, its nipple rasps like sand,
Its pores, like yours, shone with salt sweat.

Bodies in absence displace their weight,
And your smooth body, like none other,

Creates an exact absence like this stone
Set on a table with a whitening rack

Of souvenirs. It dares my hand
To claim what lovers' hands have never known:

The nature of the body of another.

'You didn't write that, did you, for me?' She looked incredulously at Rana.

'Ha, I wish! It's a famous poet from a long time ago. Derek Walcott. Doubt you've heard of him.'

'Oh Caribbean poet, right? Noel laureate.' Rubi rolled off nonchalantly. Rana was taken aback. Walcott was so much before her time.

'Ok Ms. Google! Now how about some food? Trust me you don't want to miss this jamba rice!'

Rana leapt off the bed and piled food on two plates. He wondered if it tasted the same as before but there was no-one around to decide. Rubi seemed to shrink in the bed, under the duvet, her Bambi eyes darting and uneasy.

'It's not as weird as it sounds. Try a little and then you'll be having seconds, I promise you!' He laughed as he took her plate to the bed. When was the last time he had even eaten in bed? He felt like a teenager again.

'I'm sorry I can't. It's…it hasn't been installed yet. The macerator that enables food ingestion. You know this . . . ' Rubi had her eyes screwed shut as she said these last words.

His sweet child-like Rubi.

RPX01.

Rubicon Prototype 01; an advanced prototype patented by Bot-land that was used in behavioural training for the other bots in various stages of manufacturing.

A prototype he had worked on in its early formative stage. After all, Bot-Land was a key subsidiary of Integrated Interactive Learning.

Rubi was in her final stages and only essential physical developments remained to be completed. Neural networks, breathing and touch had been perfected but ingestion, digestion and excretion were still in progress. Of course, he knew all this. But for a moment it had felt good to forget and to try and feel something instead.

*

As he spooned jamba rice into his mouth slumped on the edge of his bed, it tasted of charred sandpaper.

Like all his meals every day.

CONFECTION

Khadija Rouf

'Where are you from?

'Oxford.'

'You mean that's where you live? But where are you from originally?'

'Oh,' smile, slight laugh. 'Liverpool!'

'No, I mean, but where are you *really* from?'

This is the dance, when you want to know me, and it is well intended, mostly. What is it that you are really asking me? It isn't just about geography, is it? It's about something more, about what you see in the map of my face? My body? My skin is pale, but not quite the usual tone. What is in my name? You stumble saying it, but don't ask me how to pronounce it properly. You shorten it for me, and somehow your version of me sticks. You try to code me, work out where I fit – presumably, so you can file me in the right place in your mind, connect me to the 'proper' script.

I don't feel like playing that game today.

I smile a rictus smile. 'Liverpool,' I repeat. It's not a lie, it's just part of the truth.

There you go, you can file me under 'The North' and then

you can close the lid of that little box, reassured that you know me. I file this as 'benign', along with other words used to describe me; 'unusual', 'exotic'. I think of other attempts to place me and misplace me, and the surprised reactions of, 'No offence, you don't look like one.' I've responded to this last too frequently with the balm of 'No offence taken'. But of course, this is a lie.

You don't realise that what you have asked me has ignited memories.

Later, I go home and cook. I take a gleaming pan that pours back my own distorted reflection – dark eyes, dark hair, pale skin – and wonder if I see what other people see. I tip red lentils into this pan, hear them patter like raindrops. I rinse them, swooshing them clockwise, with curls of my hand. I sprinkle in haldi, grind in salt. I will boil them hard and the orange suns will dance until they break their own boundaries and blend into a thick, yellow sauce.

I take a sharp knife and unwrap an onion, chopping its flesh into thick, silver arcs. With the blade's heel, I crush garlic and unpeel its broken body. I heat oil in a frying pan and throw in cumin, garam masala, chilli, garlic and onions. The onions heat and gloss become translucent, sweating softly. The pan sings to me, a golden song, a song of heat and fidelity. The onions are ready, and I stir them into the lentils, a marriage of flavours.

I eat this dish alone. I eat more than I need. I taste the past in it.

*

On a glorious December day, my parents stand outside the registry office at Mount Pleasant, Liverpool. The sun casts dazzling

91

strips of light across once grand Victorian buildings, throwing stark shadows across the vast streets that echo with the laughter of seagulls. The sky is bright blue, cloudless, brisk.

Amma – though – she is not my amma yet – has found an illuminated scrap of pavement. My Abba breathes the crisp salty air sweeping up from the Mersey. Some of Amma's red hair breaks away from her carefully constructed beehive. She's lined her eyes with kohl, and holds back tears in the cold, not wanting black lines to run down her face. She's wearing the palest pink lipstick, and holding a small bouquet of red roses. She feels like a queen. Abba is wearing a black suit, shined shoes, a wool Nehru hat. It is always so cold in this city.

The two witnesses – passers-by surprised to be invited into the registry office to watch the short ceremony – gently stamp their feet for warmth. There are new rings on Amma and Abba's cold fingers. Amma's pale hand entwines Abba's dark hand. Their hearts are filled with hope, and they are laughing. Already they are three, as a tiny heart is beating inside Amma's womb: me.

The small party suddenly stands still and focuses in one direction, smiling awkwardly. 'Say cheese!' I guess they were all dazzled with flashbulb impressions hovering in their eyes, like wayward angels. The chilly breeze pricks Amma's skin with goosebumps as she obediently follows the photographer's directions. She is stilted and still, but Liverpool breezes across her wedding sari, making it flutter. It is pearly-white Damask, embroidered with silver threading along the pallu. It gleams in the sunlight.

*

This story is a confection. Amma tells me more than one version of it. The past is porous. Their wedding day photos, stashed in a precious place with holy books and prayer beads, are not to be touched unless she is there. I never thought to ask why there were only eight pictures. Most are in black and white, only a couple in colour because that was more expensive back then. I didn't notice pauses. I didn't ask why there weren't more guests. Why the only photos were inside the registry office and on the pavement. I hadn't learnt to see who was missing. I gazed at her beautiful white sari, not knowing until later that in a place where the sun rises deep red across paddy, white is the colour of mourning. Really, someone should have told her.

Years after that, she tells the story again, but this time she starts to name those who were absent – her own parents, siblings, friends. She started to say something about why they were absent. That it was 'a different time'. She would not use the ugly words for why none of them came, just that they 'didn't approve'.

I think back and wonder when a sense of difference comes. I try to imagine Amma and Abba relaxing after those stilted photographs were taken. Gathering themselves to get a cab to their new home in Toxteth. They would have blended in because the borders were fluid. But they would have stood out everywhere else. People stared, some said things under their breath. Some said them out loud.

*

Some while later, it was time for me to leave the shelter of my Amma's belly. Both our bodies were propelled into a dance, which we did not have to learn. It was already laid out underneath the breath, deep within muscles, the alchemy of hormones and neurotransmitters. I needed some help to leave; forceps ensured my eviction. I will learn later, through snatches of life that our fates lie not in our stars, but in who we are when we emerge in those convulsions that squeeze us out into the world, bloody and coated in vernix.

I think about Amma, dazed, exhaustedly looking at the baby who had just been flopped onto her chest, heavy and steaming. Perhaps she couldn't take much in amidst the noise of surgical instruments.

'It's a girl', the nurse says.

'Why is she white?' my abba says.

And perhaps that's where the trouble began.

*

The jokes last a childhood. I am not really my abba's daughter. I am a foundling. I am a sprite, a bhoot. I am the milkman's girl, I am the daughter of the chip shop owner. I am loved, but never quite one of the family. Brothers and sisters come later, darker by degrees, but still difficult for others to code, still ambiguous. We see how 'Asians' are portrayed on television – comically ineffective, sputtering, unassertive. Many of the actors are white underneath their boot-polish make up. One of my brothers decides to be Italian. Another decides to be an Arab. They shorten their names. They could belong anywhere. Khalid becomes Kal. Muhammed becomes Mo. Somewhere we learn that we can sometimes move with ease, and sometimes not. In our Nice Middle Class area, we learn that we stand out. That there is no-one quite like us. We learn that on trips out in our

94

car, we may be stopped. Abba may be asked if he owns the car he is driving. We learn that for him the world is not so navigable.

We sniff his fear but cannot name it.

I somehow weave through the gaze of other peoples' codes, sometimes invisible. I do not lie; I am simply interpreted by others. My name is shortened for the convenience of others. The usual sign that I have stood out prefaced with, 'Where are you from?' and then, *'Where are you really from?'*

*

Amma reads my first school report to Abba. I stand in front of him, scouring his face. We are in the living room. He is staring at the carpet, as though studying its swirls, listening intently. Amma and Abba are in their 'home' clothes. Amma is wearing her pinafore dress. He is wearing a lungi and t-shirt. When Amma has finished reading, Abba looks at me and smiles.

'Shabash, beti! Don't let anyone put you in a box. Study hard. Study hard. But learn to cook, beti, eh? A Bengali girl must be able to cook.'

*

I don't remember when we move to a Nice Middle Class area. But one day my parents usher me past the strange angular drawing sprayed on the front door. It is a thin shape with drip marks. It is a box whose sides have been mixed up, rearranged wrongly. It is a sci-fi spider with broken legs.

'What's that, Abba?'

I sniff their fear but cannot name it.

'Nothing, beti', says Abba. 'Go inside.'

Then, their coats become curtains blocking my view. There is brown fabric in my way. I try to peer around it, but I am held close so that I can feel cloth on my skin, the reassuring smell of washing powder lingering in the weft of the material.

As I pass, I see a small hole in the panel of the door. 'Don't touch it. Go in, go in.'

There are little bits of glitter and icicles in the hallway. 'Go in, go in.'

I feel my feet slow, curiosity all the way down to my toes; want to explore, to touch, to enquire about why the doorway is different. *What happened? Why, why?*

But the coat bundles me inside and there is more insistence as I am pushed. 'Go in, go in'. A harder voice. A voice that normally appears when I am in trouble. What have I done wrong?

I sniff their fear. But cannot name it.

*

I chop vegetables that yield their scents as I cut into them. Florets of cauliflower, slices of onion, bhindi, brinjal and cabbage. Everything smells fresh, but the onions bring tears. I finely chop ginger, its tang sticking to my fingers. I chop garlic, its piercing perfume like a medicine. And hot green chillies, sliced fine. Everything is mixed together, salted, and then left for a little while to breathe and blend. Then, I mix in gram flour, rice flour and ajwain. I mix this sticky dough with my hands, and roll small chunks of it into balls that I flatten between my palms. The frying pan heats up and I place each pakora into the hot oil where it is engulfed in hisses and bubbles. Each offering returns to me on a slotted spoon, golden brown and crisp. I lay them on paper until they sweat out their excess oil, and then eat them with chutneys and raita.

I eat them all, and I taste my Amma's cooking, her love. No plate must be empty, no cupboard must be bare. I taste my childhood again. I know somewhere in the geography of the past, there must be famine. I share a fear I cannot name. I am scared of scarcity.

*

I am a teenager looking miserably at the willowy women in the magazines. None of them looks like me.

Sometimes we drive to Yorkshire to see my aunties – so many 'aunties' that I do not understand who is related to me and who is not. They are fleshy; their skin rolls from underneath bodices and their midriffs are bare. They don't seem concerned about this show of flesh. The covering of the head is more important. They jangle when they walk, bangles ringing lightly, and flip flops gently clapping on the floors. Their hair is long and shiny with tel, sleek and greasy. Some aunties have lips and teeth reddened with betelnut and paan. They talk fast and loud, and I am lost in a sea of Bangla words.

Now and again, an aunty gets eye contact with me and offers me something to eat by cupping fingers into a cone and gesturing repeatedly to her mouth, eyebrows high.

And often a question in faltering English, 'Can you cook, beti?'

I smile a rictus smile. I am not able to cook. I am not remotely interested in learning to cook. I want to look like the girls in

Just Seventeen magazine who have dilemmas about boyfriends and which shade of eyeshadow to wear.

But I am told not to cut my long black hair. I am devastated. 'Our women wear it long,' says Abba. 'Do not cut it.'

I plead with Amma. 'It's culture', she says warmly. 'You've got beautiful hair'.

*

There is always pressure to appear different. At school, the girls with blonde hair and blue eyes are the ones with all the gifts, invited to endless birthday parties. People share their food with them. I am told, *Don't share. Do not eat what they eat. We have to eat halal.*

We pore over lists of ingredients for everything. Jelly is not halal. A lot of confectionery is not halal. This meat is not halal. This ice cream is haram. That cheese is haram. The world becomes annexed.

But our house, and the houses of my aunties, were always fragrant with spices. We eat pakora, curry, rice, samosa, chapati, brinjal, okra. My hair so often smells of spices – dhania, haldi, ginger, garlic.

I am bigger than the other girls in my class – taller, fatter. I am not nimble. I cannot play chase easily.

One day, a girl rounds on me. 'You stink of curry,' she says.

After that, I take to spraying my Amma's perfume in my hair. It is called *Charlie*, and it smells sickly sweet. I do not realise the danger I have put myself in should I go near a lighted flame.

The girl rounds on me again. 'You stink of perfume.'

*

As the years go by, I am ambushed again and again. I forget that I should be equipped, constantly vigilant. That it can come at any time, and I should not rest, even amongst friends.

We are sitting across the table. I am a guest in your house for a lunch party. I am grateful to be invited. I am facing you across your best linen. There has been warm chatter, the clinking of glasses and cutlery. We have been talking about work and life and feminism.

Somewhere in that lunch, you smile broadly. 'Have you heard this joke? What do you call a black policeman?'

I feel the gut wrench, the held breath.

I wait for the spoiler, brace for the impact. I whisper, 'I don't know'.

You roar, 'A policeman! What are you? Racist?'

You laugh hard. So very, very hard.

Is my face the joke?

I don't laugh. I know you will file me as 'oversensitive' and 'humourless'. I will be put in that box. I want to leave, but I pretend to be okay. This is a lie, to slot in with your lie. I do not know where to file this interaction. The hurt it has caused is nameless.

I go home, and though I have eaten your food, I eat again.

I make sweet gulab jamun which I once took to your house. You bit into and said, 'I don't like that'. I mix cardamom and sugar and water and tears. I blend powdered milk and flour and yoghurt. I make dough, which I fry in ghee that is as hot as my white fury. I slip the little dumplings into syrup. They bob there, and I wait a while, but eat them warm. I know later that I will regret this sweetness, that it is indulgent. But it feels urgent and necessary. I will look at myself side long in a mirror and I will disapprove. But for now, I think of my parents after their wedding, eating sweets from Granby Street stores. I think of them sweetening their lips for their life ahead.

*

Later, I do look in that mirror. It always comes to the body – what we eat, what shape we are, how much hair we do or do not have, what colour the hair is, what texture, the tone of skin, whether limbs are an acceptable shape and number. This is the body I inhabit, the skin, the shape, the size of me. Uneasy to map, but here all the same, borderless. Difficult to define in a box you want to tick.

I wonder how many hours I have spent bleaching the hair on my face, plucking the eyebrows that meet in the middle. How many hours of my life have I spent shaving the dark hair on my legs, which stands out wildly against my pale, skin. My hair is thick and black. I am hirsute.

It always grows back, defiantly. My hair has determination. *Maybe I should stop fitting into other people's boxes*

*

I remember a time beyond the photograph when Amma discovers the affair.

There is shouting and commotion. I don't understand what's happening. Then there is silence.

He is leaving to be with another woman, but she still throws him out. There is no photograph of this. His clothes are thrown into plastic bags and thrown into the street. She forces off her wedding band, her ring finger cinched at the base, changed forever. I never find out what happened to the ring. She will not say. I search for it, but it never turns up.

She cuts up all the photographs. Photos of us as a family are brutalised as he is sliced out of pictures. The pictures are clumsily butchered and we can never look at them again without thinking of her with scissors and white hot anger. Polaroid photos are split in half, as though he never existed. He is sectioned off, boxed up. These photos do not tell a lie but they tell part of the truth.

Amma throws the wedding album in the bin. She is crying when she does it. Her face is like one of Picasso's women, wrenched with grief. I wait until she has burnt out, and lies asleep on the sofa. I rescue the photos. I hide the album in my wardrobe. I take it with me when I leave home for university.

Our meals change after he leaves. We stop eating curry, pakoras, samosas, gulab jamun. Instead, we eat end-of-the-day sandwiches on special offer. We boil hot water to pour over Super Noodles. We eat endless boiled eggs with toast.

'You can call me Mum now. You don't need to use Amma anymore,' she says.

Many days, she simply sleeps for hours. Her red hair fades.

Aunties melt away, and we know it is because of divorce, because of shame.

'It's culture,' she says coldly. 'You can cut your hair'.

*

I am on Mill Bank, London. It is February 2019. I walk out of the Tate. The Don McCullin photography exhibition has harrowed and scoured me. Black and white in the past. As black and white as now.

It is drizzling, cold and grey. Misery falls from the sky.

I walk up Mill Bank, through Parliament Square. Damp flags are everywhere. Union jacks, European Union flags. People clump together, drenched in something that is not rain.

Guys in football shirts are wrapped in British flags. They are white guys, mainly middle aged. They cast stark shadows across the pavement. They stare and watch me walk by, reading my face.

One of them calls out, 'Oi, you! Where are you from?'

I code this interaction as sinister. I look away, pull up my scarf, want to weep as I pass the roses, red petals laid on the pavement. Red roses as I descend Under-ground.

I think of the roses in the photograph. My amma and abba in front of the registry office in Liverpool, full of hope on the chilly December day. I think of them, Mary and Akash. I think of them as I descend on the teeth of the escalator. It's as if I am going down into the Underworld. I think of them, as I wait upon the platform, the air dancing with soot.

So much of life is predetermined, not by the stars but by the colour of skin, the composition of blood lines. The shape of eyes, lips and nose. The tube train opens its doors and I step inside the huddle of commuters. Raindrops slide out of my hair and splash onto the linoleum floor.

Somebody should have said that in a place where the sun rises, white is the colour of mourning.

THE LAST SUPPER

Reshma Ruia

On the last Saturday of his life, Gaston Marcel wants to eat alone. There is a lull between the visiting hours at St. Teresa's hospice and he tiptoes past the nurses huddled in front of a small television set. He steps out into the yellow afternoon and hiding under the shadow of a hydrangea bush where the purple-headed blooms give off a sickly scent, he hails a cab to take him to Chez Pierre.

The hospice, in his ancestral village is his final stop, crouched in the shadow of the mountains, hugged by the sea, a small scattering of houses, a village square and a school and thanks to him, the one restaurant that had placed it on the map. Chez Pierre. He repeats the name under his breath. He came of age there and it is time now to pay it his last respect.

When he enters the restaurant, there is a scraping back of chairs. Eyes leap up, scrutinize him as he makes his way to the table by the window. He lifts a hand in greeting, throws a lopsided smile like a flag flying at half-mast before sitting down. He is a tall man with stooping shoulders and a shock of thick chemo-proof grey hair. He had been handsome once. '*Gaston, the telegenic chef of today'* was what the tabloids called him. There was the sensual pout of his full mouth, the deep cleft in the chin and a husky voice that no doubt helped his meteoric rise through the ranks, from the chef of a small provincial restaurant to fronting his own television series that beamed on Netflix from Sao Paolo to Sydney. His ratings were consistently high, especially at Christmas when he extolled the virtues of his products – pre-made mince pies and microwavable Brussel sprouts with lardon, even *Sacrebleu*, opening his restaurant for Christmas lunch. Crouching low on his gangly knees, his face flooding the camera, he told his devoted viewers to free themselves from the tyranny of the kitchen hob. '*I implore you on this one day to liberate yourself from the oppression of peeling, pruning, basting and bickering. Reach for my chestnut-stuffed goose and my truffle-smoked pate. Snuggle up to your loved ones, caress their cheeks and squeeze their hands. Let them know they are loved.'* On hearing this, the women sighed and untied their aprons and the men shifted uncomfortably in their chairs.

Chez Pierre has not changed much. The tablecloths are the same – the colour of dried roses pressed within the pages of a long forgotten book. He approves of that. Everything else about his village has changed. Next to Chez Pierre squats a video parlour and a betting shop. The road is busier too, filled with Lorries thundering past. In the time he has been away, the village had gained notoriety as the birthplace of French *nouvelle vague* cooking. Out-of-town day-trippers with bulging wallets and aspirational taste buds arrive to Instagram the latest delicacy.

The maître d' with his gelled black hair and white jacket that strains at the stomach approaches his table.

'Monsieur Gaston. It is an honour to have you with us.' He

pauses, clears his throat, lowers his eyes and continues. 'So sorry to hear about the malady. If there is anything, we can do. The restaurant is at your absolute disposal.' He waves his arm, the sweep of it embracing the restaurant with its mock Louis XIV chairs and the red velvet shaded chandeliers that swing dreamily from the low beamed ceiling.

'The malady?' Gaston repeats the word. 'It's called cancer. Cancer of the stomach – a fitting illness for a chef, don't you think?' He lifts a wry eyebrow as he shrugs himself out of the tweed overcoat that is too big on him.

The table by the window. It was his favourite. Once the last orders were finished and the kitchen restored to its scrubbed monastic purity, he liked to walk through the swing doors that separated the kitchen from the restaurant. A cigar clamped in his mouth and a glass of Bordeaux in his hand, sitting at this very table where the sunshine now pours over him like a blessing, illuminating everything. *Food is not meant to be eaten by candlelight – it can't be hidden. A good dish needs to lie in front of you, pure and naked, like a beautiful woman exulting in her own beauty.* These were his words on gaining his first Michelin star. He had banned candles from his restaurants, insisting on high voltage bulbs that lit up the food. He looks around. There are candles everywhere and fake silk orchids that bow like demure geishas in their blue ceramic pots.

'I don't need the menu. Take it away,' he tells the waitress who has placed a fat leather bound book, thick as a Bible, on the table. 'In my day I used to go to the wholesalers in Rungis, just outside Paris at the crack of dawn, sniff out the freshest meat and vegetables and then decide on the dish. The plat du jour was scribbled on the blackboard and I personally selected the wine from the cellar, the bottle still coated in cobwebs straight to the customer's table. It was all instinct, spontaneity and history. There was no need for this premeditated…' He finds he is rambling. Head in his hands, his thumb stroking his chin, he hunts for the words.

The waitress stands to attention, arms crossed behind her back, her eyes wide open, drinking in his words. She is a young girl with a shapely waist and a dimpled smile. He would have flirted with her in younger, happier times, but now he can only look at her through mucus-blurred eyes.

'The guests prefer a big menu,' the girl explains in a timid voice. 'They like to have choices.'

'Fat oil tycoons from Texas and shady Russian oligarchs! What do they know about food – burgers, potato chips and cabbage borscht!' He gives a dry chuckle. All he wants is some onion soup followed by an omelette.

The girl is surprised. 'Our specialty is boeuf bourguignon and steak tartare. We also have some fresh flat oysters from the Bay of Brest.' She rattles off the names breathlessly and then pauses, pen poised over her writing pad waiting for his answer.

'Nah, don't really care for any of those, but good try my dear. I'll stick to my order. You can tell the skill of a chef in how they handle an egg, a bunch of onions and a block of butter. That's the first lesson I learnt when starting out,' he tells her. The past is like an old VHS video cassette unspooling inside his head.

*

A memory stirs. He sees himself again, as he was, a trembling freckle-faced boy with eager hands and a thirsty mind. His father was a plumber, his mother the village seamstress. He wanted something more from life.

'I want to cook the best food in the world,' he announced one day. Their mouths fell open. Their eyes grew round like the moon.

His father shook his head. 'Cooking is a woman's job. Your mother cooks in this house. She can even make a half-decent coq-au -vin at Easter. You think you can do better.'

He had begged to differ and reminded his father that the best chefs in France tended to be male, Georges Auguste Escoffier for instance. 'There is more to cooking than potatoes, beans and chicken,' he told them. 'Have you heard of these things, do they even exist in your imagination?' He recited the names like a prayer—emerald broccoli, quail eggs that quivered with life, green-lipped mussels and tomatoes with the blush of sunrise on them. He had dreamt of preparing them, he said, in ways that would set free their soul. 'The food would dance inside your mouth, like a carnival or a wish fulfilled.' So many years had passed and he still remembered the words he had used.

The parents listened. 'The boy's gone cuckoo.' His mother tapped the side of her head. 'Food is just food, son. Something to fill your belly. We are poor folk. Don't dream fancy.' She held up her hands – plump white fingers with blunt nails and blisters. 'See these hands – they have become ugly with work. Work that will push you, our only child, to a bigger, brighter tomorrow.'

His parents visited their parish priest, their mouths sagging with disappointment. Their son, pinning his star to a kitchen when they wanted him to go to college, sit the civil service exam, join the ranks of those who owned a house with the mortgage paid and enjoyed a week's vacation on the seaside in Deauville.

He started as an apprentice with Anton, the old chef at Chez Pierre, long since dead. The restaurant was falling out of favour. Youngsters preferred to spend their Saturday nights at the newly opened MacDonald by the port, making eyes at each other over, 'so called French fries and dead meat slabs between two white buns,' Anton had snorted in despair looking at the cheap laminated menu covered in the stars and stripes of the American flag.

'I'm prepared to work for free,' Gaston told Anton, his eyes blazing with ambition. He started at the bottom, peeling potatoes and sleeping under the sink, body curled like a foetus against the cold. He was watchful, an eager student observing when the old man shelled the peas or deveined a lobster. 'Food is like a prayer. Whether it is a slice of bread or caviar from the Caspian, you must treat it with the same reverence.' That was his apprenticeship mantra.

Those early days. He had treated the kitchen like a chemistry lab – mixing, pouring, stirring till Anton had barged in and cuffed him behind the ear. 'No, no, this gooseberry jus cannot go with poussin. This is a cactus flower – it cannot be eaten or soaked in vanilla essence.' Gaston proved the old man wrong each time. He was twenty-eight, by the time he looked up and discovered his hands held culinary magic when it came to cooking. Chez Pierre gained a Michelin star and he found himself on the cover of the prestigious *Gastronomic* magazine.

Marcel Gaston remembers it all, sitting at the table by the window, waiting for his onion soup, the bustle of the diners eating and drinking around him, like the buzz of distant bees in an orchard. Their initial fascination at his arrival satisfied, they have floated back to their respective worlds, oblivious of the man who sits in their midst, a recipient of the *legion d'honneur* and three Michelin stars, his name patented on a range of sauces and dressings and his face with its blue drooping eyes fronting restaurant franchises from Dubai to Dublin.

'Still or sparkling?' The waitress has come back, holding two blue glass bottles poised over his water glass.

'The nights were always sparkling,' he replies and smiles. 'I'll stick to grapes if that's all right.' Eyes screwed tight through the reading glasses he examines the wine list.

'The cellars seem to be well stocked.' It is an observation not a question but the girl is quick to answer. 'Our Master sommelier, Monsieur Lescot, is from Paris. He trained at the Grande Verfour. He is level 4.'

Her cheeks blush rose pink with pride and he wonders if there is some form of romantic attachment between the two. Love is an occupational hazard in his trade. Young people confined together in a small space, faint with the haze of spices and aromas, heads pressed close together over a simmering pot, the arching back as one strained to reach a condiment from the shelf, a loose tendril of hair that escaped the hair netting and the soft glow of perspiration on one's upper lip. Who could blame them if their hormones swooned and rebelled? He had been guilty of such transgressions himself.

He reaches for the wine glass and takes a generous swig. He has opted for his favourite wine – a bottle of Domaine Leroy Musigny Grand Cru 2012. It is against the oncologist's orders, but he is past caring. He takes another generous sip, but he has to make an effort to taste its jewelled undertones or its velvet smoothness. The cancer has done this to him, bit by bit robbed the feeling from his taste buds so that his tongue sits inside his mouth like a dead unwanted muscle. Every morsel he takes, every drink he swallows tastes only of sawdust and razor blades. It's a cruel joke he thinks when he has spent a lifetime pursuing food that could open like a flower inside him.

The soup arrives. He stirs it, once and maybe twice before taking a slow tentative taste. The waitress bends down and whispers, 'Would he be so kind as to praise it. The chef in the kitchen was in knots with worry.'

He tries hard. Takes another mouthful, willing his mouth to respond and says he can feel the tang of the Gruyere and the onion. The colour of the broth is as it should be. But there is something else there – a certain piquancy. It is like a musical arrangement where another rogue note has altered the character of the whole composition.

He puts down his spoon. 'Call the chef. I need to speak to him,' he instructs the waitress.

The chef is a woman. She strides towards him, wiping her hands on her white apron, pausing at the tables of the regulars, exchanging a smile and a quick word, until she reaches him. Her hair pulled back in a severe ponytail, her eyes framed by large black glasses give her the air of a schoolmistress.

She bows her head, presses her right hand to her chest and stands waiting. He tastes the soup again and smacks his lips.

'This is quite divine, it's something I would have done myself. But there is a discord, a rogue element I can't quite place. Forgive me.' He dips his thumb into the bowl and sucks it, like a child sucking a pacifier. 'Forgive me, I can't identify it,' he repeats. 'I am unwell and my senses are going to sleep.'

'It is tamarind.' the chef helps him out. 'The tartness is tamarind. The scent is lemongrass.'

'A bold move,' he says. 'Escoffier would perhaps not approve but I certainly do.'

She smiles and drops him a quick courtesy.

'I learnt it all from you, Monsieur. From your cookery shows on TV. I watched them as a young girl, rushing home from school. I travelled the world without leaving my chair. You taught me how to subvert the expected.' Her words come out in a rush.

He laughs disparagingly. 'You're being far too kind. I have no time for those documentaries anymore. You fly to some exotic location, set up your table on a river bank, sharpen up your knives and some lackey grates the ginger, crushes the garlic and arranges the spices in little ant heaps of colour in terracotta bowls. You then stare into the camera and say with utmost sincerity, 'Tonight I will cook you the most authentic of prawn curries, and you stop and add a dollop of crème fraiche. *Voila*, it becomes your signature and earns you a star.' He stops and coughs into his napkin, delicate pinpricks of blood. Taking a deep sip of his wine, he continues. 'It was all a sham but it paid well. The only casualty was me, left without a wife or kids to wave me off into the sunset.'

The maître d reappears. The chef is required in the kitchen. 'If you will excuse us, Monsieur,' he says, with an exaggerated bow. 'A group of Japanese businessmen are due this evening and they have already phoned in their order. A new Toyota factory is being set up. The Mayor says it will create three hundred jobs. Save the young men running to Paris and London. Our restaurant will benefit.'

'Who would have thought,' Gaston says.' It wasn't so long ago that this was just a little coal mining town, miles from Paris, its only claim to fame being that Napoleon once got lost and spent a night here.' He stops, breathless after his long speech

111

and checks his watch. The bottle is empty, the soup bowl scraped clean. He has no appetite for the omelette that is yet to arrive. The disease has done that to him – blanched dry his every cell and pore. Curdled his insides.

The chef whispers something to the maître de and disappears into the kitchen. She comes back immediately, bearing a plate like a crown.

'I would be honoured if you tried this,' she says, placing it on the table. 'It is the first dish you prepared that got you the Michelin star. I've tried to recreate it several times. Please, it will be an honour if you taste it.'

She doesn't need to explain. He knows this dish. He is ashamed of this dish. It sits before him reminding him of what he did wrong. A plate of charred lettuce and smoked beetroot and nestled in the middle a deconstructed quail egg with gooseberry jam and a sprig of rosemary.

He waves it away. 'It tastes vile. I don't need to eat it to know it. God alone knows why they gave me a star for such absolute nonsense. Most of my life I've hoodwinked too many people too many times with food that tastes of garbage. Say it once loudly and critics will look up, say it twice with confidence and the world will lap it up. A herd of sheep, the whole bloody lot of them.'

The maître d giggles, as does the chef. They take away the dish.

The afternoon shadows lengthen. The restaurant is almost empty of diners except for a table at the far end where a courting couple sit, bodies leaning towards each other, noses almost touching. Love. The sweetness of it. The ache of it. Even now at seventy and dying, Marcel Gaston hungers for it.

He raises his empty glass to them.

MADE FROM SCRATCH

Deblina Chakrabarty

Everyone has their own version of what constitutes a 'hard question'. For me, growing up in an all-girl's school, it was: If this was your last meal on earth, what would it be? And no matter who it was, pretentious Maya, cuddly Shivani, ethereal Rhea, or querulous Tamara, the answer was some version of the same. 'My mother's *sorpotel*', 'my ma's *dal chaaval* of course', 'mummy's airy-fairy fritters'. I had to sit this one out, because by the time I had tried to find an appropriately sentimental answer, the question had moved on.

I didn't have any mummy/food memories. My mother didn't enjoy cooking. And I didn't think much of it until these questions started. And then, before I had a chance to try and convince her to start cooking if only so that I could participate in pajama party talk, she died. So that was that.

But over time I realised that the answer to this question – or lack thereof – went beyond gastronomy. It stretched all the way to the Big Stuff like family, belonging, warmth, memories, identity and every big idea debated in First Year BA Philosophy at college.

And not answering it implied conclusions about me laced with pity and insight I had no desire to hand over to anyone. Not least, the knobby-kneed boy in class who faux-worshipped Proust and silently rated all the girls in the class as if he were the chief model coordinator at Elite in the age of the 90s supermodels.

So like most things I did, I set about industriously winging the reply. Collecting artfully mismatched foods associated with memories like a jar of cowries and shells in a beach house. Bear with me if the pairing of the diverse dishes seems odd and inconsonant with the finesse of the palate. As you know, the last meal is so much more than just food.

Dark chocolate sponge cake with a chocolate ganache icing. I now live in the baking capital of the world. I am sure Paris would disagree and New York would snigger but hey, there is only one Great British Bake Off. London has found a clever way to beat the competition. Just give them a hawking spot in your town! French delicacies? Sure, no problem. Scandi chic Nordic bakeries? Minimalism, blond wood and salmon bagels, here we come. Turkish delights? Coming right up! Palestinian Berber discoveries? All hail the patron saint Ottolenghi. Turn a corner and there is a great cake waiting for you in London to accompany your coffee or cuppa.

But my tryst with the oven began a long time ago when everything about baking was wonderfully alien and fancy (unless your family ran a neighbourhood Catholic or Irani bakery). We didn't own an oven, but my friend Mira did. Our giggly chatter extended from the classroom to her house many afternoons when we had been grouped into the same projects. Her home influenced my ideas of a 'beautiful home' just as browsing Architectural Digest does today. Those days, my own house was perfectly functional and meticulously neat but there was nothing in it that could be termed décor. Mira's house contained lots of things in it that simply looked nice. Rough-hewed wood chairs in the corridor in case you wanted to chat on the phone or read. Massive Madhubani paintings occupied entire walls with moulded brass spotlights to light up strategic portions. I kept wondering where the wires were. A light emanating from the middle of the wall was sheer magic and, dare I confess, ever since then, concealed lighting has never lost its fascination for me.

As a special treat, Mira's mother would let us help her bake a cake if we finished our project on time. That was the first time I came face to face with exotic ingredients like vanilla pods and cooking chocolate. For someone whose Dairy Milk bars were rationed to one a week, here I was grating an actual brick of chocolate with a knife to produce a pile of dark chocolatey gossamer curls. Under her mother's expert guidance, a mess of flour, eggs, milk and chocolate turned into a decadent sponge of chocolate and cream

Mira and I didn't have elaborate thoughts on the longevity of our friendship. We just continued being friends through school, then college, then through art school (Mira) and regular undergraduate (me). Sometimes we lived in the same city, sometimes we didn't. Our overlapping sphere of friends expanded and shrank like the penumbra of shifting shadows. At one point I dated someone who had previously asked her out. At another point she drunkenly kissed an ex of mine at a party. Those early awkwardnesses helped us define our boundaries without having to talk about them (thank god!).

And yet, despite everything, we came unstuck over time. No confrontations, just that life got in the way. There was always something to do before we returned each other's calls. Then life's details were too much to cram into one conversation so we left out the little incidents that held the best clues to our present selves. And over time, for each other, we became frozen patinas of our youth. I missed the person she had become but there was no doorway back.

But chocolate sponge cake will always be a somnolent afternoon spent giggling with Mira as the aroma of hot cake enveloped us. Sound of Music OST played in the background on a vintage gramophone and all was right with the world.

A full English breakfast for dinner – 2 eggs sunny side up, 2 thick slices of toast, one generously slathered with perfectly creamy butter, and one with Marmite and a chunky slice of ham or two on the side (never sausage, too greasy)

I know this is blasphemy in the UK. You'll jump indignantly and tell me this is not a full English. Where are the hash browns, baked beans, grilled tomatoes even? What do you mean no sausage? You need to understand I was eating a version of full English via Persia. This is what they served in the Irani restaurant in Bombay at Fort for decades until they shut down and sold up to become a cash machine for a popular bank. I usually had their spicy mince curry with crusty buns, or the fluffy white boiled chicken sandwiches. Maybe the apricot chicken curry if I was particularly indulgent or those geometric triangular vegetable patties when in a rush.

But when I met S there after work, barely 3 months into my first job after college, it wasn't going to be a rush or a celebration.

This was a separation. After two years together, one year apart, virgin joints smoked in the haze of Pink Floyd, virgin corporeal territory also ceded in the haze of Pink Floyd, mismatched ambitions and innumerable fights ending in 'Fine, whatever', it was time to cut the cord. We knew we weren't meant for the long haul, but in the short haul nothing seemed wrong. The wrench felt wasteful, gratuitous.

I needed a hug to tell me it was going to be OK. But it clearly wasn't going to come from my usual hug supplier since we now sat on opposite sides of a separation. So, I sought that hug on a plate. The brine of my tears mixed with the salty eggs and ham created strange comfort. I probably looked manic, crying while stuffing my face, while this solemn, bearded boy-man sat looking at me with regretful puppy eyes.

In the halcyon days of first love, we had promised each other we would remain friends 'no matter what'. A month after this breakfast/dinner we ceased speaking. I have had no word or contact with him for the last twenty years. Breakfast-for-dinner on the other hand remains a source of tried and tested comfort. If I land in a strange country, it's often my first meal of choice from room service. It's also what I ordered on my first date with my husband once I had retched out all the tequila from a night of dance-like-no-one's-watching (but obviously someone is, that's the whole point of sexy abandon).

Beets – you know the vegetable, in all its forms. Boiled, raw, sautéed, pureed

So, here's the thing. I hate beets. I truly do. Nothing more deceiving than sweet vegetables. Sweet is the fruit's job so what's this confusing hijack all about? In the same vein I also avoid carrots, squash and all other members of the red n' orange vegetable basket since they all come laced with sucrose. So why is it on this list?

Because my father loved them.

A strangely sweet choice for a bitter and acerbic man.

We had the usual skirmishes in my angsty teens. But while my friends settled into placid relationships with their parents, my relationship with my father continued to flare like rabid teen acne come too late. The disagreements flew thick n' fast from his politics to my partners. Money always played the conversational closer, the joker in the card pack for Indian parents. It always wins a losing argument with their progeny.

Over time I became the sort of inconvenient woman who is a cautionary tale. Too smart, too opinionated, too loud, too modern. It was all too much for a middle-class Calcutta boy whose mother, grandmother, aunts had been silent queens of the zenana. His old patriarchy, held in abeyance by my mother, resumed its perch in his sixties and went into full-blown battle with my nascent feminism. They aren't being facetious when they say old age is like childhood revisited. We now live in a prolonged state of apartness. Unwilling to acknowledge its permanence or end it.

But I never pass a beetroot hummus in the supermarket or a beetroot salad at the neighbourhood deli without thinking of my father. I would like to try them, I really would. But I just can't.

Sushi – all handmade sushi but in particular a good gunkanmaki with salmon roe or a fatty bluefin tuna nigiri. And of course a spicy tuna n' crispy rice California special roll.
I realise this may raise eyebrows. It may sound odious, as if I've

been rolling in some rarefied privilege of warm sushi rice since birth in pre-liberalisation India where restaurant meals were Indo-Chinese Hakka noodles or Moti Mahal butter chicken at best. I can imagine the first instinct is to Marie Antoinette me but please don't! Let me explain.

The most important relationship in my life started with an innocuous question, can you send me some restaurant recommendations in LA? It was my first time in the US, and I had heard legends about its Michelin star sushi restaurants with single names, Katana, Katsuya, Matsuhisa, Sasabune, Nozawa. I also knew a single omakase might swallow my entire fortnightly allowance for meals.

He was a few years older than me. The right kind of age when a woman is in her twenties and thirties. His body is still firm and his reading list, playlist and visa stamps are everything you want them to be. The infatuation is inevitable. We met one hot summer in Bombay. He was visiting family, I was idling. There was some *je ne sais quoi* and that was it.

The flirtatious emails dribbed and drabbed over the years but eventually turned into check-ins and an exchange of food and travel trivia. I grew up and got a job and that job took me to California where he lived and worked, albeit a different city, San Francisco. He had on-off girlfriends. I chose not to keep track. It kept the flirtation alive.

I was expecting a suitably intrepid reply to my query filled with hidden delights and insider tips. I didn't expect the recommendations to come in person though. He flew down for the weekend, stayed for the week and we became Richard and Emmeline from Blue Lagoon, two changelings with an innocent primal connection emerging from post coitus to hungrily prowl the alleys of Little Tokyo for sushi bars. He taught me the intricacies of chirashi, inari, uramaki, temaki. I learnt to savour the fatty toro on my tongue, finally understanding what all the fuss around umami was all about. We dangled chopsticks, daintily sipped sake and stayed suspended in the buoyancy of early bliss like the ascending rows of bubbles in freshly popped champagne.

How I did any work to justify the raison d'etre of the trip remains a mystery to me.

We parted like once-in-a-lifetime lovers. We kept the exploding internet frequency alive and crackling with passionate emails and chats (MSN, Gchat, remember them?). Then like Laurasia gently floating away from Gondwanaland, the separation began. Marked by geographical distance, it was not visible to the naked eye. Then he left for good. A void in the ethereal world wide web.

In the absence of keepsakes, I made a totem of his absence. Sometimes I offered flowers, sometimes a voodoo doll stuck with pins. Both are proverbial, both are real. He was a delicious mouthful of toro, that's all. The memory is supposed to fill you rather than copious amounts of rice and fish itself. Too bad if you're hungry for more.

Paani Puri/Golgappa/Phuchka – round hollow semolina fritters filled with a variety of fillings such as lentils, spicy potatoes, chickpeas. Dunked with sweet tamarind sauce and spicy n' sour mint water.

It's hard to imagine but in my childhood, this was a common street food hawked on creaky wooden push carts loaded with a myriad collection of plastic containers, steel drums and little bowls made of dried leaves. A worn man with black dirt crescents around his fingernails would break each puff and fill them with the mash and tangy, spicy liquids as you gulped the previous one. The unspoken rule was that they were sold in plates of six but no order was complete without asking for the mandatory free seventh dry empty fritter. A palate cleanser, long before we learnt the phrase.

Most junk food enters our lives through the backdoors of youth, well-hidden from parents. But in my case, *phuchkas* strode in through the front door, arms linked with my mother who was their biggest fan. She didn't enjoy cooking, sure, but that doesn't mean she didn't enjoy good food!

My dad looked on dubiously as she braved mythical hordes of cholera and typhoid germs to gorge on plate after plate on family Sunday evening excursions. She introduced me to their delights as soon as she could and before you knew it, I was coming home from school with yellow green liquid drying on the white frill of my dress.

Cue to present and there are no street pushcarts in London. Nor is my mother. *Phuchkas* are now poncy starters in Indian fusion restaurants, the puffs lined up like military cavalry on canapé plates, the liquids apportioned elegantly in Borosil beakers and one of us at the table 'playing mum' and pouring them into the six puffs (still just six as if by some global puff code). But one squelching mouthful and I'm back where I started, under my mum's sated supervision and a stained, frilly frock.

*

I realise with a smile that mothers and last meals are inexorably intertwined after all.

TULIP PERSIMMON'S
HEAD-WETTING

Kavita A. Jindal

Gilt cherubs gazed down from the pale blue ceiling. Holding their dainty lyres like shields they watched Karina, stumbling creature that she was, make her entrance into the thronged ballroom. She looked up at the cherubs, murmured a hello to them, took another step forward and found that she was in a line for something. She tuned in to the conversation around her. It was the queue to sign the guest book. She worried her nail tip as she waited. Her friends, Rahul and Gavin, should have said on the invitation that everyone would be asked to write a commemorative line or two for baby Tulip. She would have come prepared.

As she neared the table she saw that it wasn't a book at all, but a long scroll of cream parchment patterned with tulips. She guessed these were hand-drawn by one of the proud dads, probably Rahul. Gavin and he were both artistic but Rahul was the better painter. The curly-haired woman ahead of her straightened up and handed her a fountain pen engraved with cobalt and gold tulips. Karina, admirer of beautiful objects, twirled the pen in her fingers, examining it and wondering at the cost of it. Perhaps the pen had been especially commissioned by Gavin.

Aware of an impatient rustle behind her she turned her attention to the scroll. The golden nib of the pen met the parchment and offered it a dot, a splodgy dot created by her hesitation. She lifted the nib and read a few of the inscriptions. The other invitees had jotted down smart and witty aphorisms for Tulip. Where had they found these sayings? Off the top of their heads? She felt the closeness of the person behind her, the shift into her space, and precipitously, she gave up, handing the fountain pen to the man behind her with an apologetic, 'I need to think of something to say.' She walked away from the embarrassment of her unexplained dot on the parchment.

Wading through the long legs and sharply dressed elbows of the crowd she got to a spike-haired waiter from whose tray she picked up a flute of pink champagne. More at ease with a glass in her hand she stood by the wall and scanned the room. High-ceilinged, cavernous and painted duck-egg blue. This building had been a duchess's home in the late eighteenth century. Restored to neo-classical opulence it now billed itself as London's most glamorous private club. White clouds bordered by gold floated on the blue ceiling above her. Those cavorting naked cherubs watched her, judging her navy pencil skirt with its red trim, and her navy velvet jacket. They could see into her useless empty uterus.

Karina's darting black eyes had not caught sight of a baby yet. Where was the guest of honour, the reason for the party? She spotted Gavin and Rahul in the centre of the room under the crystal droplet chandelier, being embraced turn by turn by the beautiful multitudes, but she was apprehensive they'd ask her what she'd inscribed for baby Tulip. Rahul would ask if she'd written something in Hindi as well. She must first sign the scroll before she went up to give them her own congratulatory hugs.

She rifled through her head for snatches of poems, quotations, wisdom. Something that would be memorable for Tulip Persimmon Dutta-McDougall. Something the girl would like to read later on. When Karina was thirteen, there had been a fashion for autograph books in her school in Delhi. All the girls had bought one and they'd passed it around the class for their friends to sign. Karina was the only one actually leaving her class that year. Her father had been transferred to the consulate in London and he'd promptly arranged for her to board at a school in Gloucestershire where she could finish her schooling regardless of his further transfers. In the first few months in England she'd missed her friends and looked often at her autograph book. She knew by heart what everyone had written, the silly rhymes, the sincere I-will-miss-you scrawls.

The boy she had liked best, the one she would love forever in her frozen memory of his boy-state, wrote: 'Have a good life.' As bald as that. She would never see him again. Nothing had spoiled the memory of her crush, not even his limp autograph. Maybe he'd grown up to be ruthless, slightly paunchy and a trifle smug, like her boss. He might have become someone she would barely tolerate, if she met him now. Or maybe he'd become a computer genius, nerdy or marginally bohemian, absorbed into Silicon Valley. No matter. It didn't concern her if he himself was having a good life or not. It was the boy-he-had-been that she loved forever.

She remembered another autograph from her book, a little rhyme painstakingly written out in elongated flourishes. It was signed by someone she'd not really noticed or spoken to in her school years. The boy was two years above, if she remembered right. She certainly hadn't asked him for a memory, but he'd somehow gotten hold of her book and written:

The grass is green/ The rose is red/ I will love you/ Till I am dead.

So far nothing appropriate for Tulip Persimmon. Karina kept the brain pages turning. Surely another glass of pink champagne, another smile from the handsome waiter would help? Yes. A poem perhaps. *What is this life if, full of care / We have no time to stand and...* no o, not appropriate. Why had she regressed to thirteen years old this evening? She should act her age; be the mature thirty-eight-year-old that she was.

'Hello, you realise you're talking to yourself – you look quite funny.'

Sahil, her husband. They pressed their lips to each other's chastely. She raised her glass. 'My fave.'

'Hmm...good. What were you babbling to yourself about? You look crazy.'

Her withering look had no effect. 'Did you see the guest scroll we've got to sign?'

At his nod, she said, 'Fantastic idea, but I can't think what to write. Why don't you sign it for us?'

No doubt he'd bypassed it as something she would do or had done. He would have started socialising already. Sahil never dithered.

'Oh no. Not me.'

'Why not?'

'Because if I do, I'll just write something banal, then you'll go over to read it, then you'll come up to me and say it's barely legible and lacks sincerity and I should've at least given it some thought and then we'll have a row.' He picked up a glass from spike-head's tray and released a 'mmmm' when he had sipped the extraordinarily buttery champagne.

'Are we having a row now?' Karina mumbled, 'because you've refused to sign the scroll on our behalf?' She was talking to herself because it didn't seem like he'd heard.

'You wouldn't think they could have it all,' he lifted his chin at the room. 'Rahul and Gavin.'

'I'm not sure they do –'

'But look at them. A baby now. A girl baby. Is that even allowed?'

Karina knew his words came out of a pit of bitterness. She was just about keeping her own jealousy pressed within. Any moment it would bubble out and a river of slick green saliva would run from her to Rahul and to Tulip, wherever she was, and Karina would be marked out as the wicked witch with ash in her soul.

She wanted to be the good fairy. She wanted to feel happy for Rahul and Gavin. For her and her husband to seem delighted. She wanted to try, at least.

'Sahil,' she said, 'They didn't choose the sex of the baby. As far as I know. I'm not sure you can. Or not in any foolproof way.'

'But that's what they wanted. And that's what they have.'

She was silent. It's what Sahil and she didn't have, despite years of trying and two cycles of demeaning treatment.

'Is Ferny here?' Sahil asked. Ferny was Tulip's birth mother.

126

'No, I don't think she's a part of tonight's jamboree.' Karina waved her hand at the well-dressed people around her. 'I think this is for the parents, the daddies. Look at their faces…how….' she stopped herself. Talking about the dads' faces was unlikely to make Sahil gleam.

'I've seen the daddies' faces,' he cut in. 'Yes, they're over the moon. I'm sure they will be wonderful parents. Tulip is a lucky girl, no doubt. But…' He frowned and his patrician nose indicated disapproval. 'Not everyone is Gavin, not everyone is Rahul. I wonder if this should be allowed?'

'It *is* 2002,' she said brightly, meaning anything could happen now that they were in the twenty-first century and all social conventions could be explained or overturned by dint of living in a new age. It was the reasoning she deployed when she didn't want a discussion to progress. She had her own opinion about Tulip but hadn't formulated a defendable argument and she wouldn't enter the fray unless she was going to win. She returned to an earlier comment Sahil had made. 'I don't think Rahul has it all.' She sneaked a look into her husband's eyes. 'His family won't speak to him or acknowledge him. They won't be mentioning *this* to anyone…'

'Huh…parents. Who cares? Look at him, he doesn't care.'

'*I* know he does. He just won't say so in front of Gavin.'

'Parents are a bother…haven't you noticed?' Sahil put on his jokey voice.

Yes, they'd had plenty of pressure put on them, and misunderstandings about their childless state.

'He's better off not caring.' Sahil's eyes wandered away from her and over her head. He was ticking off the people he knew in the room.

Karina looked across at Rahul, resplendent and perspiring under the central chandelier. Like her, Rahul was from Delhi and when they'd met at university they had bonded over early childhood memories that were similar. She knew that Rahul ached to be accepted by his family. He had told his parents a few times that he was not interested in women. They had ignored him and not enquired further. They preferred denial. Karina had met his parents once. After that she'd tried to dissuade Rahul from sharing too much of his life with them. She knew he would not be able to change their prejudices. It was better for him to accept that some people were beyond changing, they just couldn't do it. It was too much for them. But Rahul had charged recklessly into their precious peace and announced that he was going to live with his partner, had said that he was one-half of a man couple, and that they were going to have a baby. She was not surprised at the reaction from his parents.

Rahul must have sensed her scrutiny because he came towards them and enveloped them in an immense hug. 'What misery am I saving you from?'

'Arguing the demerits of parents,' Sahil replied promptly.

Rahul's eyes clouded but he continued to hold them in his embrace. They voiced their congratulations on the birth of baby Tulip, Sahil managing to sound almost as thrilled as his wife. Karina received a tender squeeze from Rahul in return for her profuse felicitations and she felt emboldened enough to ask if Baby Tulip was attending her head-wetting celebration.

'We don't want her disturbed too much,' Rahul whispered in her ear. 'You know, not too many people breathing on her, or smoking around her. She's in the small drawing room next door, with a nanny. Tell Samantha I sent you to give Tulip a kiss.

Knock on the door and say the password, Heavenly Cloud, to be let in.' He squeezed her arm again. 'Only my bestest are being given the password so don't tell anybody else.'

Karina slipped away feeling specially awarded. Sahil would be fine on his own, networking. He would find mutual acquaintances to gossip with. Everyone would be gossiping.

'Heavenly Cloud.' She knocked and giggled at the ornate door to the private drawing room. A youthful girl opened the door and giggled back at her, letting her in, and quickly latching the door. Tulip Persimmon was asleep in her baby-carriage. Her long thick lashes lay curled on her cheeks. Her tiny left hand lay on her lips with two fingers wrinkled. They must have just slipped out of her mouth. She was completely undisturbed by the hubbub coming through the door. Karina moved a chair close to the pram and carefully held Tulip's right hand in her palm. 'She's so… small', she whispered to Samantha, 'such a little person.'

Samantha nodded. 'She's just six weeks old.'

'She's adorable.' A tightness in Karina's chest.

Samantha gave another quiet nod.

'Her lashes,' Karina burbled. 'They're like Rahul's. Are her eyes like Rahul's? Sorry, I don't know if you see Tulip regularly,' she added hastily. 'Are you her nanny?'

'Yes. But at the moment both of them are around constantly. I'll spend more time with her when they start up a regular schedule again.' She smiled. 'Little Tulip does have the most fantastic lashes. Wicked.'

'Are her eyes like Rahul's?'

Samantha looked uncomfortable. 'Could be,' she replied. 'It's hard to be sure. Babies change all the time. Some people say she has Gavin's mouth and jaw. We'll have to see when she's a bit older.'

She'd been well trained. She hadn't mentioned Ferny. It was impossible that Tulip had genes from both dads. If they knew who her biological father was, which they must do, they weren't saying. Karina caressed the sleeping baby's right hand for a few minutes, idly noticing that Tulip was not a pink and white baby but olive-skinned. But then Ferny, her mother, was also mixed race. Was that a deliberate choice?

No one put these questions to Rahul and Gavin. It would be too intrusive. She herself knew all about unpleasant invasive questions. Whenever IVF was mentioned. If she raised it herself she didn't mind talking about it in detail. Other times, she couldn't say a word without thinking that she'd snap. Those were the low days. On the more normal days, she sometimes thought that it didn't matter so much, what she had and didn't have; what people asked her or didn't ask her; what they thought her choices were; what advice they doled out unbidden: eat more chillies, learn belly-dancing, get a dog. More difficult to negotiate, more sorrowful, was the chasm that lay between her and Sahil. He seemed not to know when Karina was having an overly-sensitive day. And she wasn't any better with him. They were the absolute worst at reading each other.

She must not sob in front of Samantha. She bent to give Tulip the promised light kiss on her cheek and tried to smile a serene goodbye.

On returning to the ballroom she was offered a cupcake iced with a red tulip from a laden tray. She snuffled it in two bites and slunk along the walls, towards the right of the room, feeling she ought to circulate and also make her way to Gavin, whom she hadn't congratulated yet. She brushed cupcake crumbs off her skirt. The air was thick with voices, laughter, whispers, clinking glasses and wisps of smoke. The gilt cherubs frolicking above now seemed sedate in comparison. This club was no place for a baby. Rahul must have smuggled Tulip in, or got special permission. Were babies allowed in here? She didn't know, but she found herself grinning. Now she was talking like her husband: Is this allowed? Is that allowed?

Who cared?

As she slipped along the periphery, honing her expression of enchantment, she came across a booth screened by black velvet curtains. The heavy drapes were strung on two sets of circular rods, one inner and one outer. A narrow French table stood outside the booth. A delicate white card: Tarot Readings. Karina paused. Was this the amazing reader Gavin often mentioned? The one who got to the heart of the matter and whose wisdom he trusted. Rahul had told her that they both took the guidance of the tarot reader seriously.

She peeked around the first half-drawn curtain. Inside in the shadowy light, she saw a table and two chairs, one of which was occupied by a woman whose pale hair was enhanced by the grey gloom. Cards were stacked in neat decks in front of her. A white hand lifted up, almost ghostly, gesturing for Karina to come in and take a seat. She stared at the fortune-teller, who was an albino, white-lashed, pale-lipped, and wearing a white cotton blouse. It would be rude to walk on now. Timidly, she sat on the vacant chair.

The woman stood up to close the curtains fully, the rings juddering along the rail. Her trousers were black and narrow.

She returned to the table and lit the tea lights in their glass jars. A silver bracelet with tiny green charms graced her left wrist. Flames from the candles warmed the dim space making the reader look more other-worldly than she had before.

Karina waited. The two of them eyed each other appraisingly. The tarot reader put out her hand. It was cool to touch. 'I'm Michelle.'

Goodness, she had the honeyed voice of an apsara. 'Hi, I'm Karina.'

Michelle said nothing, so Karina asked, 'Have you been busy this evening, lots of people stopping by?'

'Some. I'm a bit hidden in this corner. It's a huge room, and with all those people crushed in the middle, not everyone can see what's at this end.'

'I guess. So…'

'So…'

'Are you going to start?'

'What is your question about?'

'Uh…I don't have a question.'

A patient smile from Michelle. 'It's best to ask a particular question. That is the only way to get a relevant answer.'

Her solemn pronouncement made Karina anxious. This isn't just playing, she thought.

Her question formed as Michelle held up her palm. 'Don't tell me your question yet. Just let me know is it to do with work, family, health, what sort of thing?'

'Uh…family.' Karina looked down. *Will I ever…?*

Michelle selected a deck of cards and moved the others away. 'Hold this for a minute. Shuffle it please. Now, cut the deck and hand it back to me.' She began to lay out the cards in elegant undulations. 'Before I do the reading, I'd like to ask…how straight do you want it? The truth or just a hedging around?'

Karina considered. But again, before she could answer, Michelle said, 'My readings don't always please people. But I get the feeling you don't want bullshit.'

'No. Tell it like it is, Madame Zelda!'

The tolerant smile that said she'd heard it all before. 'What was your question?'

Karina bit it out.

Michelle squeezed up her eyes to view the cards she drew, in the way contact-lens wearers did. Her silky soft voice began the reading, pointing card by card, as Karina gazed at her fortune splayed on the table.

Eventually, the velvet curtains were drawn back to allow her out. She walked on shaky legs, not caring where she was heading, her mind awhirl. She blamed Michelle for her unsteady state, she should complain to Rahul, to someone, anyone, really she should. But she was caught up in a group now, she'd inadvertently lurched towards people she knew, to a corner where her friends were hanging out. She wasn't tall enough to have spotted them across the room before. They were deep in Tulip gossip, but for Karina the choruses ebbed and flowed as if from a distance, and occasionally the word 'baby' crashed around her ears. She couldn't concentrate. No babies. Not for her anyway, according to Michelle. It wouldn't happen. And Sahil didn't want to adopt, Karina knew that. She was going to be left childless. Was it even allowed that a tarot-reader could tell her that?

But the mellifluous Michelle had got extremely animated at the very last card, 'The Lovers', and said that Sahil and she would develop an ideal partnership, fulfilling their other ambitions and even being envied because they would have less to fret about than their peers.

According to Michelle, or according to the cards, whichever was the real soothsayer, Sahil loved her deeply, despite not showing it, despite the quarrels about fertility treatments versus adoption versus no children. That last card was a very good omen. It meant that on reflection Karina would work out that it was all for the best. Sahil and she would be a strong team.

The voice had remained musical. Had Michelle noticed how Karina's dark eyes had stayed fixed on the cards in the second row after her interpretation? She had not moved a muscle although cards had continued to be laid down and the voice had carried on its rapid interpretations. Karina's eyes had flickered only at Michelle's dramatic inhalation on the final card.

Perhaps the tarot-reader knew what she was doing. She'd tried to soften the blow. But there was such a thing as hurt ovaries. It wasn't something you could explain. An ache had started low and was spreading up and out like a tree calling for branches. It buzzed into her ears and mouth as she stood there ensconced within her womb-like group, unable to heed anything. It will take days to calm myself, she thought, days before I can hear properly, speak sensibly again.

She excused herself from her friends to steal along the duck-egg-blue walls, inching back to the guest scroll, which was fatly rolled at the top now with the last of the blank space spread across the table.

Karina picked up the extravagant pen and wrote in a trembling hand: 'Dear Tulip Persimmon, may your daddies always give you as much joy as you have brought to them.'

She stood by the doorway gazing into the room until Sahil's head turned towards her. He was trying to decipher her mood. She messaged him with an eyebrow. She wanted to go home.

He messaged back with a nod, raising his forefinger in a 'give me a minute' sign. She slumped in the doorway. He would be a few minutes.

The buzzing in her head began to die down. The buzzing was tinged with relief. She could just begin to admit it. The not-knowing was over.

Karina straightened up and then slumped again, overcome with remorse at her own behaviour. Unforgivable, she told herself.

She had reacted badly in the black velvet cocoon. Fury had got the better of her. She'd wanted to halt that melodious voice, stop it short in the midst of some reassuring phrase, wipe off the patronisingly patient expression, blow out the bloody tea lights, set fire to the halo of white hair.

She'd picked up the cards in the second row that spelt out her answer and torn them. One by one, each card ripped neatly into four pieces. She had hissed at Michelle as she left, 'Thanks, colourless person.'

THE CONNOISSEUR

Nadia Kabir Barb

The man in the ill-fitting brown suit at an adjacent table was talking in a voice meant to carry. 'Disgraceful!' he said, while trying to gauge the extent of his audience. Shamim looked up from his food as did others at his own table.

'This biriyani is disgraceful. Where are the potatoes? Is there a shortage of potatoes in Bangladesh? And I tell you,' there was a pause for dramatic effect, 'This,' he pointed to the platter in the centre, 'wasn't made with ghee.'

A harassed-looking young man hovering nearby came running. 'No, no, uncle, I assure you we used ghee. Let me get you more potatoes.' His eyes darted to the guests seated around the other tables to see if they were listening. He was obviously a member of the bride's family, given his deferential demeanour.

'More potatoes? Ha!' His eyes were round with exaggerated incredulity. 'There wasn't even one.' The uncle, who Shamim inferred was a guest from the groom's side, looked to his companions for affirmation. Some bobbed their heads in agreement, others looked away in embarrassment or gave their attention to the much-maligned biriyani.

The young man clicked his fingers to a bearer holding a jug of water in one hand and a few precariously balanced empty plates in the other. 'Hey you, go and get a dish of hot biriyani. Make sure it has lots of potatoes. Go. What are you waiting for?'

The bearer nodded and scurried off in the general direction of the kitchens.

Shamim witnessed the scene unfolding and shook his head as he took a mouthful of said biriyani. He hoped his vociferous neighbour would pipe down before any more attention was directed towards him. He was used to being party to some form of drama at the weddings he had attended, not all the weddings, but enough to make him relatively untroubled by it. If it wasn't the food, not enough potatoes in this case, it was the bride fainting during the ceremony due to the heat, the groom's party arriving late, hostilities ensuing because the bridal party was not adequately obsequious. It added a little spice to the festivities but this loudmouth was too close for comfort. The sooner Shamim could eat and go the better. He chased the last few grains of the polao around the plate before scooping them up in his spoon. He would have used his fingers but given everyone else was using forks and spoons he resisted the temptation. It was inherently more satisfying than using these metal utensils.

The man next to him, sporting an impressive handlebar moustache underlining a bulbous nose leaned in, 'Can I pass you something? More biriyani? Some salad?'

'No, no, thank you bhai. I'm full. Leaving space for the mishti.' Shamim said, patting his stomach and wondered what had engendered this sudden show of consideration. They had barely exchanged more than the obligatory greeting since they had taken their places at the table. The attention was unwelcome. His eyes

137

followed the man's gaze as he glanced over his shoulder to the table with the disgruntled guest. Shamim assumed the man thought he was part of the groom's entourage. To his relief and that of his companion, the man in the brown suit was tucking into a plate of biriyani with gusto, temporarily appeased by the pile of potatoes heaped on his plate.

Shamim was sitting with a group of the bride's relatives. He gleaned this information from their few attempts at conversation, asking each other about some mutual relation or their respective health. They were quite the motley assortment. Opposite him was a middle-aged couple who said nothing but ate enough food to put Shamim's appetite to shame. There was the moustached man and his wife who disconcerted him somewhat by smiling benignly at him throughout the evening. There were two young women who were the daughters of the middle-aged couple and giggled more than they ate. Both were wearing brightly coloured, matching saris, one emerald green embellished with gold, the other a vibrant turquoise and gold, with a dazzling glut of sequins. Shamim's two-year stint working at a sari shop, amongst other jobs, gave him the ability to identify both the type, quality and price of a sari. He pegged them as good quality, mid-range georgette ones. Every now and then the duo would whisper something to each other and peek at him under their long lashes and he couldn't help gazing at them in admiration. He did, however, make sure that their parents were giving the food their undivided attention when he smiled back at them, not wishing to incur their disapproval. Next to the middle-aged man was someone who looked familiar. The slicked back hair, the black rimmed glasses. He couldn't quite place him. It would come to him when he wasn't trying so hard to think about it.

His eyes scoured the hall to see if dessert was imminent. The army of waiting staff were otherwise engaged as they ferried platters, jugs and plates through the maze of tables.

The Jasmine Wedding Convention Centre was abuzz with the sound of gentle conversation. A new structure in the Dhaka skyline, it boasted three different halls of varying sizes. Shamim viewed the vast hall with approval, the largest of the three and his favourite. It could accommodate most guests in one sitting, unlike some of the other venues where you had to eat in batches. The raised dais at the far end of the room was bedecked in flowers, weighed down by the assortment of multicoloured blooms, much like the diminutive bride with the multiple necklaces hanging from her neck. Just the value of the jewellery on her person would be enough to set Shamim up for life.

He picked up his glass of borhani, taking a sip of the thick greenish liquid. As a child he had found the spicy yoghurt drink distasteful and wondered why anyone would choose to drink it. But over time he had acquired a taste for it, even the pungent smell of the Himalayan black salt or bit lobon. These days biriyani without a glass of borhani felt incomplete, and it helped him digest the rich food. Recently he had attended weddings where people had served fizzy drinks with the food. Even the thought was sacrilege and made him baulk.

Two bearers clad in their white uniforms and turbans arrived in due course with trays and placed the small clay pots of firni on the table. The first mouthful was an explosion of flavours. Shamim closed his eyes in reverence. It was exceptionally good firni. He used his spoon to scrape every last bit of the saffron-infused rice pudding into his mouth. He could have eaten a couple more but there didn't appear to be any extras.

His belly was full, but it had not been a satisfactory evening. The uncle had been right. The biriyani must have been made with oil, or the ghee was of an inferior quality, and there was a distinct lack of potatoes. Biriyani without potatoes was sacrilege. Shamim had become quite the connoisseur over the years.

He thought of Haji Shaheb who would have raised his hands heavenwards in despair had he been alive. As a child, Shamim had lived down the road from 'Haji's Biriyani' in Old Town Dhaka, considered the best in the city with people coming from all over. The goat meat would fall off the bones and melt in your mouth while the rice was fragrant with ghee and saffron. The potatoes were always piping hot and buttery. Despite his ever-growing reputation and the demand for his food, Haji Shaheb only ever made two large pots of biriyani a day and when they were finished, he closed shop. He didn't do it for the money, he would say. People were forgetting their roots and their cuisine with all the new restaurants sprouting everywhere in the city serving Chinese, Thai, Italian, Korean and what not. Even biriyani was being bastardised, he used to lament.

'I'm so sorry, but I don't recognise you,' the middle-aged man said as he pushed away his own empty bowl, 'Age is making my memory weak. Are you from Jalil's side?'

Shamim looked across at the man with strands of hair combed over his balding pate. It was a polite way of querying Shamim's presence at the table. 'Yes, I'm his second cousin from his mother's side of the family. Shamim.' He placed his right hand over his heart, tipping his head in a show of respect. The whole table was now looking at him with interest.

'I'm Farah's uncle, Asadur Rahman. And you are…?' This was directed at the man with the black rimmed glasses. 'Also from Jalil's side?'

'Ji,' he nodded. Not a man of many words, thought Shamim.

'Achcha so you two must be related?' This came from the moustached man's wife.

Shamim and the man with the glasses exchanged a glance. The man answered, 'I'm Jalil's cousin but from his father's side of the family.'

'Very nice to make your acquaintance.' Moustache man said. 'I am Belal and this is my wife Fatima. We are neighbours of Faruk bhai and Seema bhabi. Wonderful news about Jalil. We just heard from Faruk bhai.'

There was silence from both Shamim and Jalil's cousin. 'Yes, indeed. We were all very happy to hear it too.' Shamim felt the perspiration forming on his upper lip as he spoke.

'Farah is such a lucky girl. I've known her since she was this big,' the wife said, placing her hand level with the height of the table. 'Did Jalil say how long it might take to sort out the formalities?' Her large eyes were agog with curiosity. To his frustration, the bespectacled man stayed quiet.

'I don't know but hopefully not too long.' A stab in the dark. This would be a prudent time to leave. It was fast becoming an interrogation. He debated how best to extricate himself from the conversation.

'It was a pleasure to meet you all. I'll take my leave if you don't mind. Very early start tomorrow,' said the man with the glasses, as if reading his mind. He pushed his chair back and stood up. His lips creased into a smile. Shamim almost recoiled at the sight of his teeth crammed together, jostling for space within the confines of his mouth. Was it possible to possess more than thirty-two teeth?

'Yes, I should be leaving as well.' Shamim's chair scraped the floor as he arose. The girls seemed piqued at his sudden announcement, their smiles receding. He would have liked to stay a little longer and play the cat and mouse game with them since it wasn't often he received attention from girls as pretty as these two. At the sari shop, the women barely registered his presence, let alone looked at him as a man. Unsurprising as he spent most of his time with a sari draped over his shoulder trying to convince potential customers to purchase Rajshahi silks, kathans, Dhaka Jamdanis, georgettes or whatever fabric he was displaying. He was still, to his mother's disappointment, unmarried at the age of twenty-three.

Shamim raised his hand to bid them all goodbye and strolled with studied nonchalance towards the exit. He spotted a table on the far right of the hall where they were serving tea and coffee and wondered whether he could make a detour and get himself a cup of masala tea. Coffee after biriyani would have Haji Shaheb rolling in his grave.

Many moons ago, Haji Shaheb had caught Shamim scavenging alongside the alley dogs, through the boxes that had been thrown away behind his shop.

'What's your name?' he asked in a gentle voice. Shamim had bristled. Pity. He didn't want other people's pity.

'Shamim.' He had looked at Haji Shaheb defiantly. Hunger had no pride, and he felt no shame taking the discarded food.

'Wait here,' Haji Shaheb said and disappeared inside his small eatery. Shamim had waited obediently and with trepidation, expecting some form of punishment for trespassing on Haji

Shaheb's property. Later he wondered what had made him stay rooted to the spot rather than running away. After a few long minutes the old man emerged from the doorway with a box in his hand.

'Take this and come back next Friday.'

The smell wafting from the box had been like the smell of heaven.

Every week after that, he had given Shamim a box of biriyani to take home to his mother and younger brother until Haji Shaheb had died of typhoid years later. He had also taken Shamim under his wing and given him a job at his restaurant at weekends serving customers, though it had come with the condition that Shamim continue his schooling on the other days. This kindness Shamim had never forgotten, nor the taste of proper biriyani.

Haji Shaheb's face was as clear to him now as if he were standing before him. He could visualise his white cotton pyjama and white kurta, the tunic grazing the top of his knees. The embroidered cap he wore on his head and his beard which Shamim had watched turn from grey to white. After his death, his sons had taken over and expanded the shop. They had even opened one in Gulshan where the elite of Dhaka society resided. They also started cutting corners using inferior cuts of meat and adulterated ghee, letting him go when he had voiced his concerns. He wondered what Haji Shaheb would have made of that. Now, opening his own biriyani shop was Shamim's dream and an homage to his mentor.

Except for the firni, the food tonight had been disappointing. Despite wanting to finish the evening with a hot cup of sweet tea, he decided it was wiser to depart before being caught. He smiled at guests as he neared the doorway waving his goodbyes to random people. Some raised their hands in response, most had blank, confused looks on their faces.

He stepped into a blanket of humidity as he emerged from the cool air conditioning of the hall. The man with the glasses was standing by the gate next to the security guard who was stretching his arms as a yawn ambushed him. Shamim stopped a few paces behind in case the man engaged him in conversation and questioned him about the groom or his family.

'Bhai, is there a wedding here tomorrow?' Shamim overheard him ask.

The guard nodded, 'There are three tomorrow evening sir.'

'Till tomorrow,' he said as he patted the guard on the back. Shamim smiled. He knew where he had seen the man before. They had both been present at two other weddings, one in this hall and the other at a venue two roads away. A fellow wedding crasher.

He made a mental note to stay away from the venue for the next few days in case their paths crossed again. He just hoped the biriyani next time would be better than Jalil and Farah's, cooked with proper ghee and with an abundance of potatoes. The way Haji Shaheb would have made it.

FAST WITH A PURPOSE

Mona Dash

1 – Home, Bhubaneswar, India

Alisha watched her mother slice a red onion, pale-pink smooth slivers fanned out on the chopping board. Her fingers moved at a furious pace as she continued what she was saying, 'Naisha's flight arrives around nine in the morning. Your father will go with the driver to pick her up. Such a pity she hasn't been able to come with her husband like always. Raja had to travel for work. But still, this time you are here! For the first time, both my daughters at home for Savitri!' Rajshri sniffed, and smiling broadly, tossed the onions into the waiting wok. The pool of oil sizzled obligingly, and her bangles tinkled with the energy of her movement.

Alisha merely grunted in return and sipped her orange juice spiked with vodka. Duty free vodka – only two bottles of alcohol allowed per person – still in the depths of her suitcase, taken out surreptitiously and poured into a glass when no one was looking. In the living room her father watched the news about the hurricane ripping through America.

'Good thing Alisha is safe,' Pradeep announced, as if she wasn't there. Her father, plump, balding, sat all hunched up, worried about her sudden appearance in their home without Paul, but making a pretence that he was perfectly comfortable about it.

'Ma, you still do this Savitri stuff and now, even Naisha has become so ritualistic?' Naisha, so like a perfect daughter-in-law. She lived with her husband's parents and his younger brother, in a joint family set-up whereas Alisha felt a compulsive duty to smirk at anything vaguely traditional. Though she was the elder by four years.

Alisha's memories of the Savitri Puja went back as far as she could remember. Her mother, like all other married women, observed a fast and prayed to the Goddess Savitri for the long life of their husbands. Though the tradition had been changing and nowadays women could eat fruit during the day, or even a simple supper if they couldn't cope with a complete fast. Their mother would wear a beautiful new saree. She would bear a brass tray decorated with flowers, fruits, incense sticks and a burning diya and would offer it to their father, as if to the gods, then bow down and touch his feet. As little girls, Alisha and Naisha watched this ritual. Alisha, almost every year, would challenge her. 'But, Ma, why do you have to touch Bapa's feet? Why do you have to fast?' and her mother would reply, 'It is self-sacrifice. We women deprive ourselves to make our prayers more powerful. Touching the feet of elders, or anyone, is a sign of respect.'

'Then why doesn't Bapa do the same?' Alisha asked now, years later, still not accepting.

'Because, Alisha, as I have told you before, women are more powerful than men! We embody Shakti. What we pray for today will manifest tomorrow. Therefore it is the woman who needs to pray for her husband and her family.'

146

'And if they don't, then the husbands will die a premature death? What about married women from other parts of the world?'

'In North India, they have Karva Chauth.' She turned to Pradeep who was beginning to doze off. She never called him by his name. Her requests to get his attention were just sounds.

'So husbands live longer when the wives practise this whole fasting business. Isn't this illogical?' Alisha persisted.

'Aeii, please don't fall asleep like yesterday!' Pradeep sat up and mumbled that he wasn't asleep, he had merely shut his eyes for an instant.

'Sorry, Alisha, what did you say? Of course, of course, poor souls, if everyone knew the power of self-sacrifice, then half the world's problems would be solved. Divorces, accidents…'

'Ridiculous! Such rubbish, Ma!' Her mother was wrapped in her traditions and customs, unchanging in her ways. No idea about women being independent, instead of silly creatures praying for their men. Even as a child, Alisha had wanted to escape from this world, even as a child she had always argued with her mother.

'Don't laugh at age old wisdom, beti,' her mother said, as calm as ever. 'Now let's have dinner.'

Alisha sat nursing her glass, knowing here at home no one would point fingers, no would disturb her cocoon, her parents' concern soothing her. Here at home, she could be herself. In their little flat in New York, from where they could see Central park if they leaned out of the large bay window in the living room, she had yearned for this haven. The sprawling bungalow of her childhood, the busy kitchen with its smells, plain white rice cooking in its steam, mustard seeds sputtering and dancing in oil, her mother's non-stop clucking, her father's wry one liners.

147

The sense of security and acceptance. The fact that she did not have to prove herself or establish her identity here. Home. The cut-throat ambition and drive of New York, a far cry from this gentle comfort of home. The desire to come home to India had hit her as intensely as the desire to leave it.

What a cliché I am, she thought wearily. Three wonderfully busy years, and now here I am in my parents' house with a lost job and a lost marriage.

'This Dorian hurricane isn't getting any better,' her father, now wide-awake, announced from his sofa. 'Hope Paul's OK. Hope he's not travelling?'

'Everyone's fine, I am sure. Manhattan isn't affected at all, Bapa.' Was he trying to find out what had really happened? Had Ma coached him to be diplomatic? And what if anything did happen to Paul? How would anyone know where to find her? No one knew that she and Paul had split up and she had fled to India.

'Naisha will decorate the deity. She'll tie a saree around that pestle, put some sindoor on – beautiful! She's so much better than I am!' Her mother and father were always like this, both talking about completely unrelated things, neither answering the other. Like now – her mother's eyes shining with pride at Naisha's skill while her father watched the news oblivious of his wife's comments.

'Kusum aunty, Sneha aunty, Sucharita, Rachita, and some of our neighbours whom you haven't met yet will come home in the evening. Everyone is so happy to meet you, Alisha!'

'You aren't implying that I need to be actively involved in this puja stuff, are you?'

'Why not?! Just because Paul isn't here, doesn't mean you

won't join your own family.I have a new saree for you and everything.'

'Ma, I have been married for four years now and I never do Savitri. Work is busy, meetings, travelling. I can't fast. As for touching your husband's feet! Are you all aware this is the twenty-first century? What happened to education? Isn't that Rachita a surgeon? Even she is doing this ancient Savitri puja?'

Her mother looked up from laying the tablemats, bright pink flowers on a blue base. 'Every married Odia woman observes a fast on this day for their husband's long life, so you need to as well. Even if your husband is an American, it doesn't matter, in fact all the more reason you should.'

'He needs extra redemption does he! What a bother! Oh all right, whatever, I will do it,' Alisha said, realising she sounded just like herself as a teenager.

Later, in bed, she felt furious that she had given in. Given that Paul might not even remain her husband, did she have to go through this farce? She had blocked him on WhatsApp, and kept her phone switched off but she couldn't resist checking his Facebook, just a quick peek. No update for a fortnight. His profile picture was still of them, standing close, all smiles and embraces.

Before she ended up writing to him or liking some old post, she got off Facebook and idly googled the legend of Savitri. She reread the details, how Princess Savitri fell in love with Satyavan, how they got married, and finally how she saved her husband from Yama, the lord of death. A strong intelligent woman, Savitri overcame death itself. 'But in doing so, you spawned a tradition of wives fasting for their husbands. Well done, Savitri!' Alisha said aloud, shutting down her laptop.

She thought of the first year after her wedding, when her mother had emailed her instructions about the Savitri puja and the fast, but on that evening, they had been invited to a friend's for dinner. Paul laughed when she mimicked her mother's panic as she ate canapés, and as always, his blue eyes lit up, his face crinkled like bright wrapping paper. A sight she loved, a sight she now missed.

2 – Home, New York

Over time, things had changed. They started to argue. Lazy, from her, disorganised, from him. She complained he spent too much, he told her to stop nagging. He started returning home later and later. And talked a lot about Olivia, one of his colleagues. She remembered Olivia as the flirty blonde she had met at his office Christmas party, and then one evening she had seen them together, in a little Italian restaurant, just as she turned into 32nd. Like a couple on a date, on one of the outside tables. A checked tablecloth and a little red rose in a crystal vase. A glass of ruby red wine and Olivia serene in a light pink dress. Paul had turned and seen her. 'Alisha?' But she had fled.

He returned that night, after the dinner, eyes stony, 'What on earth was that about? Why did you run away? How embarrassing!'

'For you or me?' She asked in disbelief.

'Me of course. Instead of coming over, you scooted like a rabbit. Olivia will think my wife is insane.'

'It doesn't strike you that it's odd to walk by and see your husband sharing a cosy meal with another woman?'

'What do you take me for, Alisha? She's just my colleague. It was a work thing.'

'Then why didn't you tell me you were meeting her?'

'I did say I would be late.'

'At work, Paul, at work, not schmoozing with some girl.'

'Anyway, why were you there? You were following me. That's why.'

'I wasn't. Just a wrong turn.'

'A wrong turn on the way home?'

'Come on, you know my sense of direction! I can get lost anywhere.'

'And why were you walking in those shoes?' So he had noticed her high wedges.

'I couldn't find a cab straightaway, good weather, felt like a walk.'

'Lies, lies! You followed me. You don't trust me at all, do you?'

They fought all night, accusations pouring without respite. Things started crumbling, like cookies left uneaten for days. They managed to stay out of each other's way. Paul's business trips got longer.

A week later, she lost the multi-million dollar deal she had been working on and her boss called her in. Granted the economy wasn't doing that well, but the enterprise security market was still growing so there was no excuse that she was only at fifty per cent of her sales target. He discussed an amiable 'parting of ways.' Human resources soon came around to sort out a severance package. 'I met my targets consistently for the last three years and had this deal closed, I would have smashed it again,' she said, but Kevin had shrugged his shoulders and mumbled, 'Sorry, shit happens, life…'

She had walked home from the office in a rage, tears wild on her face, and before she got into their empty flat, she'd bought a ticket to India on her phone. She'd packed a bag hastily and left a post-it on the fridge. 'Goodbye Paul. That's it I guess.'

3 – The day of Savitri

Alisha couldn't sleep. She couldn't stop thinking of him, his touch, his smile. Not just him, of herself, smartly dressed, rushing into the office, making her commission, best sales person last year. All of that was lost. A mirage now. And she could tell no one. Her parents would be upset and break, like glass.

It was almost dawn, the sky blushing a light pink, when her eyes finally closed. She woke when the sun poured through the deep green curtains. She could hear sounds from the kitchen. Her stomach was uneasy in this set up of extensive oil and extra food. If only she could get some fresh bagels and a nice Starbucks. But Starbucks hadn't yet heard of Bhubaneswar, this sleepy town, deep in eastern India.

Some excited voices and high-pitched laughter floated up. The doorknob turned, and Naisha came in, dressed up in a cream and red saree, and a blaze of gold jewellery.

'Ohhh Didi, you are still in bed?! Come on, you need to shower. We need to set everything out for the puja. Then we'll go to the temple, and then to the shops. I need to get some bindis and bangles to match my other saree, a beautiful silk…'

'Whatever happened to a plain old Hi??'

Naisha laughed as if that was the best joke on earth. 'How American. Hi indeed. Come on, come on, wake up!'

'Any chance of a skinny latte somewhere while you buy your bangles and stuff?'

Again that loud laughter falling out of her. 'You are so funny, Didi! How's Paul Bhaiyya?'

'He's fine, I expect.'

'Ufff, so formal.!' Naisha dragged the cover off her, the room quite cold with the air con on. The familiar arms, the loud exclamations, her sister so very cheerful, her mother so conservative, her father so tranquil. She was powerless to resist the gaiety.

Pradeep had brought most of the fruit market home. There were mangoes, sweet, small and juicy; bananas, yellow and shining; watermelons, cut into red quarters; guavas, with pink insides, pomegranates broken into pink pearls; fruits chopped into fruit salads and fruits left whole. There was a special dish of moong dal soaked overnight, mixed with milk, bananas and sugar. These would be offered to the goddess.

Alisha dressed in the bright pink and yellow saree her mother had given her and even found an old blouse in her wardrobe to go with it.

'Oh, this blouse still fits you? How do you keep your figure? Look at me, one year after marriage and I need new blouses.' Alisha felt her sister had a course in histrionics. Naisha batted her eyelids and smiled a yearning smile, old movie style. Yes, she looked decidedly plump. The New York women would shrivel before her buxom self.

In the afternoon, people started arriving, the women dressed in colourful sarees, shiny gold jewellery, the men content in the knowledge of being prayed for by their wives.

What a carnival, Alisha thought. If only she could message Paul. *Here am I stuck with these Christmas trees in the bright sun, help!* He would laugh and they would kiss, and the world would be set right again. But there was no Paul. There would be a divorce. But she couldn't stay in Bhubaneswar forever, could she.

She would have to go back to New York, restart, find herself a new job.

'Love conquers all, even death.' Her father's voice came from the living room 'Sri Aurobindo writes it in this epic poem, Savitri.' He held up a thick volume. 'What Savitri demonstrated was her intelligence, her devotion, her prayer. That power can't be underestimated!' He read some verses out loud to a rapt audience.

Love conquers nothing, love is transient, Alisha thought. Hadn't Paul and she been in love? But how quickly it had disappeared! Small problems of living together, a difference of cultures, personalities.

The women sat in a semi-circle in front of Naisha's homemade deity and chanted the 'Savitri brata katha', the whole story of Savitri. They sang together, their voices, their hearts in agreement. The deity was dressed in a red and gold saree, her gaze at once benevolent and searching. Wherever Alisha turned her head, her large eyes followed. She stared at it and somewhere inside her a question formed – 'So do I lose my husband just because I never believed in you and your fasts? Is this my retribution for mocking you?'

All the women around her were ululating, eyes shut, hands folded in prayer. Alisha didn't know how to do that, but she folded her hands, shut her eyes, and prayed. Just once, let me see him again, even if only once. I miss him. They rang the little handbells. Incense sticks and diyas burned bright.

'Rituals are observed by human beings because we have no other way to express our faith in God. But God doesn't punish us if we don't observe it! He is fine if we just believe, if we have faith,' her mother often explained.

Maybe the goddess wasn't out to ensure she was subjugated,

maybe she could actually help, protect Paul from hurricanes and women like Olivia, protect the love she felt for him? This incense and chanting are getting to my brain, Alisha thought. I am losing myself in this chaos. Sleepless and dazed, I am not even rational.

Indeed she *had* followed Olivia and Paul that day. She had arrived in his office, all dressed up, to surprise him, thinking it would be like old times when they did things on impulse. They could go up the Empire State building and stand in the same spot where they first met, when she had bumped into him taking selfies. Then dinner in a little seafood place she had booked.

Outside the office building, she had seen Paul and Olivia walk past, and instead of coming up to him, she had followed, unobtrusively. Not that they went far, a little Italian one block down. From across the street, she had watched them settle at the table, and imagined occupying the table next to them where she would stare straight into Paul's eyes, until he admitted his guilt. Unfortunately he had suddenly turned and seen her. And she fled.

Paul hadn't even tried to deny it or apologise. Her marriage was over. Just like the job.

The puja over, her mother asked, 'Are you hungry Alisha? You know it is OK nowadays to have some fruit, or some puri.'

'I am fine, not hungry really.' Food was far from her mind.

'I knew it! Love keeps you safe. When you make a gesture like this for your husband, you don't even feel hungry. Prayers work.'

'Wish someone would pray for me.'

'But I do. I fast for you once and for Naisha once, every year.

155

On separate days. You can do the same for your children, when you have them, I mean.' Her mother and her logic! All these women blindly believing in something, hopelessly dependent on their husbands. Desperately wishing she had a cigarette even though she rarely smoked, she went up to the terrace. Maybe the clear air would cool her head. She sat down in a corner of the terrace and leaned against the parapet. Dusk brought with it a nice cool breeze, soothing after the heat of the day. Night was falling and the first bright stars were twinkling through. When young, she and Naisha often spent evenings here with their father. The first star was not a star but the planet Venus, their father had said. When she had mentioned this to Paul, he said it was this intelligence, these random facts she knew that attracted him. And her smiles, her hair, her cheeks, lips. He had smiled at her as they sipped Prosecco on a terrace bar. If only she could turn the clock back and change everything. Run a soft hand over all their fights, kiss him and watch his magnificent smile appear.

She heard some excited shouts from downstairs. What a merry crowd they were, people without a care or worry. She was tired. Not used to the incense, the smoke, the scents. If Paul was here, he would be curious about everything. He would ask about Savitri, why they worshipped her, and she would laugh at his tangible Americanness, his attempts to find a parallel. He would say he hadn't had vodka or sushi for a whole day. Wasn't that self-sacrifice?

Alisha's thoughts blurred. Even as he was talking, he was beginning to disappear, fading out. She called out to him. She ran looking for him. The house she was in was not theirs, and she couldn't recognise where it was. So many trees, like redwoods, like oak, huge trees surrounding the house, and she was running into the rooms looking for Paul. Finally, a closed door which she pushed through. And he was on the bed. A woman with him, on him. A tattoo spun across her back, butterflies in flight, exactly like the one she had always wanted, Paul's fingers laced in it. 'Olivia?' she asked. But then the woman looked up and smiled. It was herself. The girl was herself.

In self-sacrifice there is a power. In faith there is strength. Paul was whispering to no one else but her.

Suddenly there were voices. 'Of course something is wrong. The way she arrived, all of a sudden without Paul. I always worried, marrying an American…'

She woke up. Her parents were standing at the door to the terrace. Her mother was talking rather loudly, as she did.

'Oh Alisha, you are here? We came up for some fresh air.' Her father was so bad at being diplomatic. The worry on his face was palpable. They had surely come looking for her.

'It's much nicer here,' she said, 'Such a clear sky tonight.'

'Let me get my telescope. And do you know you can even see the Lingaraj temple from here?'

A temple town, they called Bhubaneswar. Sacred, holy, beautiful temples. Gods of various names and forms residing in each of them. Paul had always wanted to see more of India. They had planned to see it together. One day.

'Telescope! Why are you talking about telescopes?' Her mother sounded incredulous. She was nudging her father, 'Remember what you were meant to ask?'

And as always her father, clearly uncomfortable at being coached, began. 'You know Alisha, since Paul is not like us, I mean, an American, we were wondering if I could talk to him… are things between you, I mean…'

At this point, a scream. Then Naisha was on the terrace too, breathless. 'Didi, come downstairs, come. There's a call for you. Quick come, come, it may get cut. Paul Bhaiyya. Come.'

'Calm down, Naisha,' she said.

They followed her down the stairs.

Downstairs, the phone was in the living room. In the corner, the deity in front of the phone was still staring at her. At the other end of the line, what was Paul doing? Was he in their wooden-floored living room, looking out of the large window as he waited for her to answer? She picked up the phone, aware she was alone, but sure they were listening outside the door.

'Yes, hello?' she said, freezing her voice, deadening it.

'Darling,' a whisper. 'May I come to see you?'

'I am in India.'

'I know, I have called your landline, you've switched your phone off…But I have to see you. I have been thinking. This is hardly the way, without a word. Just this is it?'

Something in his voice. The incense burnt. The deity stared, then a flower dropped. Not one of the large oversized red hibiscus which was toppling over but a small white-petalled flower, jasmine. A pot of jasmine trailed from her balcony in her central park apartment.

'When were you thinking of?' she asked making a mental note to mark next year's Savitri on her calendar. Nothing as elaborate as her mother's or Naisha's puja of course, but just a prayer, just a fast. For both, by both.

CUFFLINKS

Khadija Rouf

Link 1

Bright and shining, forged from rose gold, they are almost solar. The handmade ingots clip his crisp white cotton cuffs together. He looks at the gold cufflinks, glinting in the silver surface of the mirror.

He inspects his reflection, holds his wrists up, near his face. He raises an eyebrow and smiles.

'Mine,' he thinks. 'Mine.'

The small lozenges rest on his sleeves – their twin surfaces gently undulate into billows and swirls, and are set crisply with the brilliance of small, milky pearls. The sway of the gold reminds him of wheat waiting for harvest. It is bountiful, promising bread filled with the taste of sunlight and the glory of long summer days. These yolky gold cufflinks glimmer so softly. He remembers buying them in Milan. He smiles – they were deliciously costly. He lowers his arms, and stares at himself in the mirror. He adjusts his blue silk tie, ready for the day ahead.

Mercurial, Edward sweeps into the Boardroom meeting. The pebbles at his wrists power his smile. An understated statement.

He touches his cufflinks as though they are a charm against this corporate world. The faces in the audience look like sprays of flowers, lilies of the valley. They anticipate what he has to say.

He begins. He hears his own voice, smooth, molten. His arms sweep easily across his slides, projected onto the white walls. The story he tells, in his PowerPoint presentation, is cinematic. He honeys his way around his forecasts and projections. Numbers and technicolour graphs promise upward trajectories of wealth. He feels the swell of excited silence before him, and as if by magic, a generous slice of viscous sunlight pours itself into the room.

The light catches on his cufflinks, and the shadowy white walls are dotted with dancing golden droplets. They are like small, erratic confirmations of everything he asserts. They spot the cheeks of eager faces with light. *Perhaps there is a little over promising,* he thinks, *but all my lies are little and white.*

'Everything is possible,' he tells his audience. 'Everything's optimistic. The future is bright.'

He knows he has hit the right note. The alchemy of his words is met with applause. He seals the deal.

That evening, he marvels at how he moves with such ease, from skyscraper to opera. He has money and culture. He's changed into formal wear, but kept the cufflinks which brought him fortune. He makes small talk with important people he knows. He skims across the surface of everything, the world illuminated through champagne bubbles. Their laughter is weightless. Unnoticed waiters anticipate their gestures and, at the right moment, they are offered platters, bright with canapés. There are delicate assemblies of delicious food; smoked salmon, cucumber, and horseradish cream. There are wild mushroom arancini with basil pesto. Later, desserts magically appear; exquisite lemon tartlets shine on slate plates. Opera cakes, slick with chocolate mirror ganache and decorated with whispers of gold leaf.

A woman in a deep amber satin dress leans forward to eye his cufflinks. He feigns surprise and then smiles.

'They are stunning,' she says, as she sees her face reflected in their contours.

Pleased, he lets her look. He tells her something of Milan, the designer show. Just a little, not too much. He doesn't want to appear cheap.

He flirts a little, gilds his words.

Her lips glisten, responsively, they stretch into a smile.

And he wonders whether…but the performance bell sounds. And then someone is stepping in, gliding an arm around her waist. She is with someone else.

No matter, he thinks, *there will be other opportunities.*

Later, in the perfumed, half-darkness, he listens to the soaring notes of *Das Rheingold*. He is one of the audience now, part of the elite. He remembers the faces of *his* audience that day. He is pleased, he is blessed, and he is gifted. They were in awe. He smiles to himself, touches the cufflinks, strains to look at them again. He breathes easy.

What's reflected in his cufflinks is either invisible or he's chosen not to see…

Although the fates are capricious, this gold holds a memory.

Link 2

Although the fates are capricious, this gold holds a memory.

This gold holds a shadow, which fell from the brow of the person who held it, long before now. Someone mined this metal

161

in the dust and the heat. No boardroom, no pay rise, and can't afford to eat. Faceless, voiceless, he's ceased to exist. Each day, life on the line, safety risked.

Asjad digs in the dust with the heavy pick, his lungs sinking silica. He is deep in the pit, deep in the mine. There is the half-darkness, the sour perfume of stale sweat and hot dust. He has no idea how long he has been down here, disoriented by the shadows, robbed of sunlight. He feels like it has been hours, but it might only be minutes. He tries to sense his own body, to mark the time. He is thirsty, but can't tell if he is hungry. In the pit of his belly there is stone, in his mouth there is grit and rubble. He wonders where the small nuggets will go. They will never belong to him.

'Mine?' he thinks. 'What is mine?'

He feels utterly alone.

There are heavy loads to bear in the clanking heat. There is dust upon dust. There is blood on his feet and cuts on his hands. His throat is so dry.

But there is relentless digging and sweating and aching until there is ore. He fills sacks with stones, and shoulders them into the sunshine. He feels reborn as he blinks his way back into daylight. The blue sky stretches wide above him. Tonight, it will be filled with starlight that he will be too tired to see. He walks quickly, the weight upon his shoulders. When the sack is dropped, he stretches out into a new, standing shape, and looks around at the beautiful, golden earth. It is hacked, and tented, and the ponds around him are mercurial. He sees no reflections in the cloudy water. The machines crunch and grind. Rocks become stones, stones become grit. The teeth of the machine break everything down.

The particles are scooped into a crucible and swirled by hand, as though for alchemy, for magic. He works now to find fine gold particles, glittering dust. This prize slowly reveals itself, it gradually emerges from the ground down, broken rocks. Asjad holds his breath. It is dizzying. He knows what he breathes is not good.

Next, the burning – a shimmering bond is forged with mercury. Substance fires into liquid and toxic perfume. It purifies; it sheds dirt and grit; it loses its pollutants and rises, phoenix flamed. Asjad holds his breath. It is hard to breathe. He dares to hope that he has found enough. It is like the promise of summer, after being in the underworld of gritty gloom.

He inhales, relieved. Even though what he breathes is not good.

Amidst the noise of the mine, amidst the pain, he still dreams of school.

He dreams of throwing down the pickaxe forever. No more. He yearns to hold a pen, to write in books and read and get a good job where he is treated like a man. He dreams of freedom from this unrelenting cycle of digging, shouldering, searching, panning. He wants to be free of endless labour, where he is paid nothing but small notes for gold.

He dreams, he dreams, he dreams…

He's fourteen.

He is surrounded by other children like himself, digging for ore, and swirling the muddy waters in their bowls for gold.

He walks home exhausted. He gives the crumpled notes to his mother and she holds them close to her chest and thanks him, blesses him.

They sit and eat, breaking off nuggets of ugali, the reassuring texture of maize, dense and filling, even though it tastes of so little. He dips it into the thin stew. His mother has made it spicy; it will be more filling that way. They talk about how times will be better. He will save money for school uniform, for books. She puts her hand on his back, gently, full of a mother's love. Her hand is warm, reassuring.

Asjad feels his tired muscles relaxing. They talk about how things will be better. God is great, the future is bright.

In the days before the mine, Asjad had tasted school. He has read about gold.

Gold, the gift of magma. Gold, the gift of the water bearer, forced through heat and pressure. Molten metal bursting into fractured seams, cooled into veins. Fine gold particles, glittering dust. Now he is an 'artisan'. He labours for it, dreams about it, troubling dreams that haunt him with dust and crying. He fears the darkness of the mined earth. The mines are like wounds in the soil, fragile, ready to collapse. He dreams of gritty gold, swirling through burnt orange waters, laced with mercury. Gold, revealing itself like droplets of sun. It burns into purity. He sees his face in pools of gold, he sees himself drowning in its burnished glow.

In his dreams, and in his waking, this gold is never his. He is given crumpled notes for his labour. He will never be able to afford the metal he mines.

Gold. It sails away, over billowing waves, into a skyline filled with pure sunshine.

But no amount of fire can stop it being dirty.

Although the fates are capricious, this gold holds a memory.

Link 3

Although the fates are capricious, this gold holds a memory.

In the city, streetlight pools on pavements, like dirty gold.

She trudges through the pelting sleet, wet and cold. She's remembering graduation day, her parents' pride at her First. She shudders. She worries that she's wasted all that hard work…

Her horizons had shimmered with promise, the future seemed bright. But what followed tarnished her hopes. Spending day after day, endlessly staring at screens. Sitting up into the night, screens illuminating her face with mercurial light. Spending day after day, endlessly applying for jobs and writing CVs, which she became sure that no-one would read.

I may as well put them in the junk box myself, she thinks.

She felt tied to her computer and phone, constantly watching job alerts – adverts which opened and closed within minutes, up against an algorithm, which closed after the first fifty, hundred, one hundred and fifty applicants pressed send. She would nervously type, striking the keys furiously, trying to get in her documents before the deadlines shut her out. She was desperate to be scooped into the net. She prayed that she would stay connected, that the Wi-Fi wouldn't cut out. She felt caught in a lottery of youth. Lottery, but who was winning?

She started to feel invisible and spectral, gauzy and viscous; like nothing she did made any impressions on the world around her.

So she was grateful when the Designer called her, offered her an internship. She was elated to be offered a post, even unpaid. It'd be great experience. She was in awe; she felt she had been saved. This was a chance and surely better things would come…

Now, seven months in, she is walking home in the dark. She can't afford the bus fare. She is struggling to afford food. There's nothing to eat in her fridge, in her cupboard. Her savings are already spent. Her parents, who love her so much, are now struggling too, as they help her to pay her rent. When her amma calls, she doesn't know what to say. She doesn't want to worry her, so she pretends and says, 'Everything is okay. There'll be a contract around the corner, recognition for my work.' She bites down on this lie, and it is bitter.

Internship hardship, because there is no pay.

The Designer breakfasts out. He is tired after a late night of schmoozing and networking. He orders espresso and pastries, fruit salad and Greek yoghurt. Whilst eating, he writes notes, ideas for the season ahead. He is tired, he can't think. He feels the weight on his shoulders; people want fresh ideas, new classics for a new season. Everything must be seen to last, be classic, but also disposable. Here is the artistry.

He tries to remember the interns – several. He is struggling with their names. Perhaps this is something he can delegate to them. It will be a good project for them, great experience to have something which bears his brand. He will ask them, they will be grateful.

So, the Designer arrives with sandwiches and drinks, tosses them down on an office table. There is a scramble, and not quite enough to go around. The other interns have got there first, as they often do. And as is often the case, the Designer brings in food that is haram. She tried to explain once, but he simply stared, unconnected, uncomprehending.

Zahabiya says nothing now. She drinks black tea. She is patient.

*

The Designer says, 'We're doing a show. I need designs by tomorrow.'

'Yes, of course,' Zahabiya says, brightly, wreathing her desperation in smiles.

She remembers that she is doing this to get a foot on The Ladder, to get a job.

The other interns make their sketches, and then one by one, they melt away.

Zahabiya stays until nine o' clock.

She's the last person in the office. She finishes the drawings for her design; chain cufflinks, fashioned from golden swirls, set with pearls like drops of moonlight. Gold swirls, billowing and flowing like pure honey. Like the sway of wheat, waiting for harvest. Bountiful, promising bread, tasting of summer on her tongue. Loaves of fresh bread, honey, filled with the taste of wild flowers and sunshine.

She leaves the designs on her boss's desk. They are neat, with her carefully hand-written notes. The drawings are signed with her name. She arranges it and rearranges it. *Make it look neat, make a good impression*, she thinks. She feels so proud, as though golden orioles are fluttering and singing inside her chest.

And then she remembers she is hungry. It is beyond time to go home. She walks alone in the dark, and her spirits begin to sink. She buys pot noodles, pours boiling water on the dehydrated nuggets of food, waits for them to soak and swell. She miserably twirls her fork around the noodles, eating in front of 'Nigella' on television; she tries to imagine eating the dishes she sees on screen as she takes each mouthful.

Night melts into day and she's soon back again. The Designer doesn't ask how late she stayed, how she got home. He doesn't know that she walked back alone. He has no idea that she walked in fear, late at night. She walked alone, the darkness illuminated with pools of streetlight, shining like dirty gold on the pavements.

Weeks later, he calls her into his office to have a look. Opens the presentation box but warns her not to touch. Gilded pebbles, her design fashioned in cool gold, bearing the waves and furls that had flowed from her imagination, like wheat fields swaying in a summer's breeze, set with pearls like the drops of her tears.

'I wanted you to see,' he says.

She feels a swell of pride, her breath catching, fluttering in her heart. He has used her design!

But he says nothing more. No words of congratulation. No mention of a contract, no mention of pay.

Then suddenly, he announces that he's off to Milan for the catwalk show. He doesn't ask Zahabiya if she wants to come along.

He doesn't tell her that the price is high, but she's worked it out. She looks at the company website. There are the cufflinks, beautifully photographed on a backdrop of brilliant white marble. They are retailing at six thousand pounds. She searches for her name. It is not there. She cannot breathe.

The design is mine, she thinks.

'The design is mine,' he says, over drinks.

While he's away, overwrought, Zahabiya clears her desk.

'That's the last he'll see of *me*.'

She is incandescent, she is burning bright. She remembers what her Grandmother used to say, 'Sometimes people's worth is only seen clearly from a distance.' She is clear. She will go home to her parents, and she will work it out from there.

A week later, there is a text message on her phone. He has spelled her name wrong.

He asks, 'Where the hell are you?'

She deletes his message, blocks his number.

Although the fates are capricious, this gold holds a memory.

Link 4

Although the fates are capricious, this gold holds a memory.

The Designer gets the catwalk photo-shoot, he gets the glory. But behind the façade of glitter and glamour, the narrative is tawdry.

Too-thin teens clomp down the runways in too-high shoes. Discordant music echoes around the venues, the sounds reverberating into corrupted melodies that become an agony of fairground noise. Cameras click under too-bright lights, everything bleaching into agonising white. Someone takes the Designer's photograph, his arms encircling the tiny waists of two models. They introduced themselves brightly, but he's forgotten their names. Close up now, he can see the protrusions of their collarbones, their cheekbones jutting out like marble cliff edges, their eyes bright aquamarine. Somewhere around here, he knows there will be a chaperone. He also knows that after a certain point in the evening, they tend to disappear.

The Designer asks the photographer to WhatsApp him the photograph. When it pings onto his phone, he is disappointed. Breathing heavily for a moment, he sees how pallid and bloated he looks next to the girls. *No matter*, he tells himself. He is a man of *substance*. He tweets out the photograph from his various social media accounts, all under disguised handles. He praises himself, praises his brand, praises the show. When he checks

169

back in moments later, he smiles as he watches the number of hearts and retweets climb.

Edward sits in the audience, flicks through the catalogue. He feels just a little bit smug to be here in Milan. Just a little bit excited to spend money, just because he can.

He is here alone. He has decided that he deserves a little luxury.

He chooses the cufflinks fashioned in gold. He likes the design, how it billows and swirls, set crisply with the brilliance of pearls. He knows that gold will never lose its value. It is responsive, appreciative. He devours the theatre of the collection shows. The lights shine bright, the spotlights pool like puddles of gold around beautiful creatures, gliding down the runways in silks, linens, feathers and velvets. They are adorned in diamonds, pearls, silver and gold.

He does not see the misery behind the carnival. The spectacle, behind which there is hunger and sadness and dust. Here, in the atrium, there is art and artifice. Important people are sending messages, staring up and down between their phones and the stage. Important people are sending photographs, making notes, writing copy. There is noise, bustle, there are handshakes and air kisses and laughter. Here is where money is showing how it dresses, who it eats with, who its friends are. This feels like the centre of everything, and Edward is in awe. He smiles and knows that this is the first of many opportunities.

The Designer hears the cufflinks are sold. The Designer is pleased. He and Edward talk after the show, words that skim over a glittering surface, never going too deep.

'The design is mine,' he says, over drinks.

They feign getting to know each other, through talking about their work, their contacts, where they live. Everything is code for wealth. They say nothing of their friendships, nothing of their families. The contours they show each other are smooth and gilded. They bathe in the warmth of their golden glow; they reflect each other's surfaces. Everything is a transaction, everything is trade. The price is high, the notes are hollow.

The Designer feels like he has the golden touch. He tells Edward that this collection is named Midas. He laughs, heady with his own wit, his gift for commerce. The Designer spots the models from the earlier photo shoot, says to Edward, 'Would you like to have some fun?'

Edward looks at them, then back at the Designer and says, 'How old are they?'

The Designer lets out a dazzling laugh. 'They're old enough to be modelling in Milan!'

He calls them over. He introduces Edward, and asks their names again, immediately forgetting. Edward remembers: Phoebe and Xanthe.

The Designer beckons the waitress with her tray of champagne. He politely hands them delicate flutes, and then talks about his brand, his designs, how important he is and how Edward is important too. The girls smile lightly. This is their first show. They have come through the same agency. It is very exciting. There is more alcohol. The party grows louder, and then there is a DJ and dancing and colourful lights. Edward is dancing close to Phoebe, circling his hands around her tiny waist. The Designer suggests they go back to his hotel room for drinks. The four of them walk the short distance to the hotel, laughing, drunk, heady. It is a warm night, the city glitters.

The hotel room is plush, and the Designer puts on music. He opens a bottle of vodka, another of champagne. The girls say they should probably get back to their hotel. The Designer persuades them to stay. The mood shifts, no longer jovial but mercurial. There are suddenly sharp edges. Somewhere in the night, the drunkenness tips into cocaine. The Designer rubs it onto Xanthe's lips, and then pushes his finger into her mouth, rubbing it into her gums. She is very drunk. Edward is drunk, but he sees.

He looks at Phoebe, and asks, 'Want to try some too?'

She is silent. He thinks she gives a slight nod, and so he kisses her. He smears her lipstick, takes his thumb and finger and smears her red lipstick across her face, feeling powerful, drugs kicking in. He doesn't notice that she holds her breath, she is shutting her eyes, and her mascara is running.

The Designer has disappeared into the bedroom, pulling Xanthe behind him. The rest is a blur of colour, sex, booze, more cocaine. In the morning, Edward wakes up on the sofa, cold and hungover. He hears the Designer snoring in his bedroom. The models have gone.

Edward gathers up his things and leaves too. He will email later, to confirm details of when he can expect his purchase to arrive. A few hours later, he is aboard his flight home. As the plane rises, he stares at the clouds below, savouring the tastes of his hedonistic weekend. He daydreams; he anticipates other opportunities.

Although the fates are capricious, this gold holds a memory…

Link 5

Although the fates are capricious, this gold holds a memory…

The first link, and the last, is steadfast and honest. It remembers boiling seas. It has seen what was and what will come to be.

Memory forged as tectonics shift, and power forces magma to push through grit. Genesis of precious metal, through the labour of heat and pressure. Platinum white notes sear through earth, pulsing from within the earth's core. Elemental, fire brandished in water through basalt, forming ore.

Gold: gift of magma, gift of the water bearer. Molten metal is forced into fractures, cooling into veins. Gold waits inertly, staying hidden in basalt. It holds its memory, ever fixed, with truth and fidelity. Fine gold particles, glittering dust. It remembers each beginning and its memory is rich.

This gold knows that Heaven is placed in the soul where love swirls, billowing and flowing like pure honey. That love is like the sway of wheat, waiting for harvest. That love is bountiful, promising bread, promising the sweetness of summer flowers on the lips and tongue. Promising healing.

This gold knows that the Earth is a quintet of dust, and it patiently waits for the sixth. It knows that what is past is present is future. It weeps for the corruption, the mining of its soul. Each extraction brings rebirth, forced through the dance with mercury.

Alchemy makes this gold a messenger. It sighs for each Midas, drunk on fool's gold, high on the mirages of fame and wealth. It sighs for a world where people can be bought and sold. It sees their griefs, it feels the tears of the injured, their salt is in the earth.

This gold knows that peace will come, and it will be treasure.

Although the fates are capricious, this gold holds a memory…

THE WHOLE KAHANI

Reshma Ruia is an award winning author and poet. She has a PhD in Creative Writing from Manchester University. She is the author of *Something Black in the Lentil Soup*, described in the Sunday Times as 'a gem of straight-faced comedy' and *A Mouthful of Silence* which was shortlisted for the SI Leeds Literary Prize. Her work has featured in British and International anthologies and magazines and commissioned for BBC Radio 4. Her debut collection of poetry, *A Dinner Party in the Home Counties*, won the 2019 Debut Word Masala Award. Her short story collection, *Mrs Pinto Drives to Happiness* will be published in October 2021. Reshma is the co-founder of The Whole Kahani. www.reshmaruia.com

Kavita A. Jindal is an award-winning poet, novelist and essayist. She is the author of *Manual For A Decent Life* which won the Brighthorse Prize and the Eastern Eye Award for Literature. She has published two poetry collections: *Patina* and *Raincheck Renewed*. Reviewers have said of her recent writing: "witty and wry, with a steely heart" and of the novel: "the book's boldness, beauty and courage are utterly seductive." Her work has appeared in anthologies and literary journals worldwide and been broadcast on BBC Radio, Zee TV and European radio stations. Kavita is the co-founder of The Whole Kahani. www.kavitajindal.com

Mona Dash is the author *of A Roll of the Dice: a story of loss, love and genetics* (Linen Press, 2019) which won the Eyelands International Book Awards for memoir and *Let Us Look Elsewhere* (Dahlia Books, June 2021). Her other published books are *A Certain Way, Untamed Heart* and *Dawn-drops*. Her work has been listed in leading competitions such as Novel London 20, SI Leeds Literary award, Fish, Bath, Bristol, Leicester Writes and Asian Writer, and she is widely published in more than twenty anthologies and international journals. A graduate in Telecoms Engineering, she holds an MBA and also a Masters in Creative Writing with distinction. She works in a global tech company and lives in London. She was recently commissioned to write a short story for the long running BBC Radio 4 short story series. www.monadash.net

Radhika Kapur's work as a copywriter has won awards at Cannes, One Show, Clio and Asia Pacific Adfest. She was shortlisted for the Bristol Short Story Prize, 2020, longlisted for BBC's Drama Scriptroom in 2017, the London Short Story Prize in 2016 and won third place in the Euroscript Screenwriting

Competition in 2015. Her short fiction has been published by literary journals and in anthologies. Radhika has completed an MA in Screenwriting from Birkbeck College, University of London.

C. G. Menon is the author of *Fragile Monsters*, (Penguin), one of Telegraph's best novels of 2021. She has won the Bare Fiction Prize (2017), the Leicester Writes Prize (2017), The Short Story Award (2015), the Asian Writer Prize (2015), The TBL Short Story Award (2015) and the Winchester Writers Festival award (2015). She's been shortlisted for the Fish short story prize, the Short Fiction Journal awards, as well as the Willesden Herald, Rubery and WriteIdea prizes as well as the Fiction Desk Newcomer award. Her work has been published in a number of anthologies and broadcast on radio.

Deblina Chakrabarty is a freelance writer and a Bombayite who relocated to London six years ago. Since 2005, she's written for various publications in India including Times of India, DNA, Man's World and various other Dailies and magazines. She's primarily interested in the chasm between genders, cultures, cities and lovers that form open terrain for the curious examinations of her pen (well, keyboard). By day she flirts on the fringes of storytelling, working for international distribution at a major Hollywood studio.

Nadia Kabir Barb is a journalist and author of *Truth or Dare* (Bengal Lights Books 2017), a collection of short stories. Her work has been published in international literary journals and anthologies such as Wasafiri, The Missing Slate, Six Seasons Review, Golden: Bangladesh at 50, and was a winner of the Audio Arcadia Short Story Competition. She has an MSc from the London School of Economics and London School of Hygiene and Tropical Medicine and has worked in the health and development sector in the UK and Bangladesh. She is currently a columnist for the Dhaka Tribune.

Khadija Rouf writes poetry and short stories. She has an MA in Poetry from Manchester Metropolitan University. Her poetry has been published in Orbis, Six Seasons Review, Sarasvati and in the NHS poetry anthology, *These Are The Hands*, edited by Katie Amiel and Deborah Alma (2020). She won joint second prize in the Hippocrates Poetry and Medicine Prize in 2021, and has previously been longlisted in the Manchester Fiction Prize. She is a health worker.

ACKNOWLEDGEMENTS

This anthology has taken shape during the pandemic with its challenges and constraints.

The Whole Kahani is grateful to Lynn Michell of Linen Press for her continued support and enthusiasm for our writing in its varied forms.